His Majesty's Brig Alert

by

Richard Testrake

Dedicated to my wife Peggy, my daughter Lisa, and my son Charles

Many thanks for their help, advice and encouragement.

Table of Contents

CHAPTER ONE

The prize-brig 'Droits du Citoyen' of fourteen guns, swung around her anchor in Portsmouth Harbor. Her captain was a teen aged master's mate who had been placed in command of the brig by his father, a full captain in the Royal Navy. Because of the lack of more qualified junior officers on the father's frigate, the young master's mate was given the command on a strictly temporary basis lasting only until the brig reached safe harbor.

However, Mister Timothy Phillips, set upon by an enemy schooner larger than his own command, was able to instead capture that vessel and report to Vice Admiral Sir Charles Cotton with a useful prize in trail.

Sir Charles had emphasized to young Phillip's father that he disliked nepotism, but recognized success when he stumbled across it. Deciding young Phillips should have some recognition for his feat, he assured all that he was not going to give Phillips a commission.

For one thing, he was too young, for another he had not taken his boards necessary for such a promotion. However, it was perfectly acceptable for master's mates to command small vessels under certain circumstances.

Therefore, he announced he was going to purchase the brig into the service as a dispatch vessel. Normally, such brigs were commanded by experienced lieutenants, but Admiral Cotton was going to stretch a point by giving it to a master's mate.

Vice Admiral Cotton, after sending Captain Phillips on his way, addressed the lad. Fixing young Phillips with a penetrating stare, he advised. "Phillips, do not think I am doing you a service. You have shown you are an intelligent and enterprising young man. I have no doubt that given a little time, you will pass your boards and gain your commission in the usual way."

"The course you are on now, though, is fraught with risk. You will be faced with all of the difficulties more senior officers face when assuming command. However, your ability to overcome such difficulties will be lessened by your minimal rank and status in the service."

"Knowing this, understand that I do have an officer here in the flag who could stand a year's seasoning while commanding such a brig as yours. If you wish, I could place you here in the flag as master's mate and give the brig to my officer. You would be closely observed by ship's officers, and their judgements forwarded to me. At the end of a year, I might consider giving the vessel back to you. What do you think?"

"Sir, I am of course, at your command. I will cheerfully obey the orders that are given me. However, if given the choice, I would prefer command of the brig."

"Very well, Captain Phillips. It shall be so. Somewhere here I have your statement of condition. I will have someone go over it and decide what men and supplies you will need to be provided. For one thing, that name 'Droits du Citoyen' must go. 'Citizen's Rights' will never do for a King's brig. I will have Flags look up a good replacement."

"Go back to your brig, and get her prepared for a voyage to the Baltic. You will need to drop by Portsmouth on your way. I have dispatches for the port admiral there. You may as well accompany your father on his way back. Someone will bring over the pouches and the paperwork pertaining to the brig's commission. Now, if you will excuse me, I have a fleet to manage."

Tim was pulled back to the brig in its only boat, a small dilapidated cutter that had evidently once served with a fishing vessel of some sort. It certainly had the proper odor. It had been taken with the brig and there had been no opportunity to have her made to look as though she belonged to a man-of-war.

Coming on board with no ceremony, Tim called all hands. There were few enough of them. A dozen seamen and a boy were what he had at the moment. During the recent action, he had more hands, but they had been returned to HMS Resolve, his father's frigate, from whence they had originally come. He himself was the only person aboard able to navigate. On the way down to Portugal, he had merely followed his father's frigate. Soon, he must manage on his own.

With everyone on deck looking at him questioningly, he gave them the news. "Men, Admiral Cotton has seen fit to confirm my appointment as master's mate and placed me in command of the brig. He is purchasing her for the Royal Navy. We will follow Resolve back to Portsmouth, where the brig will be commissioned, then leave on a voyage to the Baltic."

Phillips looked at his crew. They were mostly seamen, rated either able or ordinary. The boy was a thirteen year old lad that had come aboard his father's ship in Portsmouth, looking to secure a place to sleep and something better to eat than what he had been existing on most of his life.

The young master's mate was going to have to take this brig to sea, away from any possible assistance from people that he knew. With no superior officer on board, he must be responsible for all that occurred. Some of the men he knew well, having supervised many of them on the Resolve, a few were strangers.

One of them, a former captain of the foretop on the frigate, had been brought down from aloft due to an injury to his arm. Jack Rodgers had been a solid, respectable petty officer, old enough to be able to bypass the more juvenile antics of other members of the crew.

Tim first read aloud the orders giving him command of the brig, then gave the speech he had listened to his father give several times on his own ships, dismissing all except Rodgers. Asking him to come aft, they stood near the tiller, idle now with the brig at anchor.

"Rodgers, we are about to sail, as soon as the dispatch bag and mail comes aboard. We will follow Resolve back to Portsmouth, then sail for the Baltic. I have nobody on board at the moment to second me. What would you feel about being appointed Bosun's Mate?"

Rodgers looked deeply concerned. Bosun's mates, among other duties, administered the punishment when the captain ordered someone flogged at the grating. A hatch grating was stood upright against a mast, the victim fastened to it and the petty officer laid on the cat 'o nine tails on with a will.

"Oh sir, I wish you wouldn't do that. I have no wish to be the one flogging a mate at the grating."

"Rodgers, I doubt there will be much of that on this brig. There are few enough of us, and it is my wish that the men, especially you oldsters, will take a hand in curbing the actions of some of the younger ones. You and I know a master's mate of my age, with a small crew, cannot command a vessel by flogging men at the grating every day. It is my hope that any men needing punishment can be punished by the loss of tobacco or grog."

"As for flogging, I give you my word that I will not order you to flog any man. Now, will you serve as bosun's mate?"

"Aye, since you put it like that sir, I'm your man."

The brig dutifully followed HMS Resolve to Portsmouth with no untoward incidents. A suspicious small ship, probably a corvette, did become curious, but upon seeing Resolve's force, wisely sheered away.

On reaching safe harbor, the brig's crew was hopefully awaiting a run on shore. Phillips addressed the men. "I know how anxious you men are to go ashore. You and I both know that is not to be, and the reason for it. The brig is seriously undermanned, and you have been working very hard to keep her up. I hope to obtain more people here in port before we leave. In recognition of your hard work, I will take you off discipline for the time being."

"How long that will be depends on the port admiral, and when he tells us to sail. You may not leave the ship, but you may invite friends and relatives aboard. I sincerely hope none of you will embarrass the ship or myself."

Captain Phillips took Rodgers aside. "Mister Rodgers, since we have no other officer on board, will you set an anchor watch? One man, perhaps with the boy to run any messages. Should I be needed, a shout will fetch me. Try not to disturb the hands at their holiday, but they must not wreck the brig."

Phillips went to the signal locker himself, and after studying the signal book, pulled out the flag hoist for 'Ship not in Discipline'.

During wartime, with a crew that had mostly been pressed against their wills, it would be nearly impossible to grant shore leave. Had he done so, a majority of the men would have simply walked away. After weeks or months at sea though, it was necessary for the men to have some sort of release. Most captains would do as Phillips, simply hoist the signal, and stand back and observe.

Theoretically, wives were allowed to come aboard and be with their husbands. However, unless those wives lived in or near the port, it would be difficult or impossible for them to appear before the ship left. Therefore, women who had merely assured the anchor watch their husband was on board, came onto the ship and made the usual financial arrangement with the man who would be her 'temporary husband'.

Some men, long in the Royal Navy, were said to have 'a wife in every port' around the world.

He had gone into the tiny cabin to begin reading over some of the papers he had been given aboard the flag, when he heard the watch hail a boat. The reply startled him; "Intrepid!"

This could only be the captain of a nearby 64 gun third rate coming to visit. He threw on his best coat and hat and ran out on deck. There were no Royal Marines aboard, of course, but Rodgers was there with a bosun's pipe he had somehow located, and four of the crew had been pulled away from their 'wives' for side boys. The greeting for Captain Wilson was certainly not 'Man o' War' fashion, but it apparently answered since Wilson came aboard with a smile on his face.

Adjourning to the cabin Tim asked the captain to be seated. "Captain, I am here to set a value on the brig so that Admiral Cotton will know how much he must pay for it. I saw your 'Out of Discipline' hoist before we set out, but my visit could not wait. No need to disturb your crew at their recreation."

Looking around at the bare cabin, Wilson wondered. "I know you have had no chance to go ashore to secure cabin supplies. Were there no such aboard when you captured the brig?"

"Yes sir. I had all ship's property not immediately needed put into storage. I understood it was necessary to set a value on everything aboard."

"You are perfectly right, Captain Phillips. However, sometimes we may put a looser interpretation on matters. Sometimes for example, cabin stores may have been damaged in battle, or through improper storage by the enemy. Sometimes, seals may have been broken, and it will be necessary to either use or discard such items before they spoil."

"I think I understand, Captain Wilson. If you will excuse me."

Tim approached a narrow hatch and opened it. On one side of a bulkhead, cases of wine were stacked. Beside them, small casks of preserved provisions were piled. In the rear were a few heavily salted hams and several sides of cured bacon hung from the overhead.

Pulling out a case of wine with some effort, he staggered over to the table and set it down. Using his new sword, he pried off the top, and extracted two dusty bottles.

Another hatch, when opened, revealed place settings, silver and glasses, all secured tightly in place. After some searching, Tim found a cork screw. While he was searching for some glasses that were not overly dusty, Wilson pulled the corks from the bottles.

Pouring the wine, he remarked, "I gather you have no servant, Captain Phillips?"

"Sir, I have a dozen crew and a boy aboard the brig. I really did not feel I should use one of them to wait on me."

"I see. Once I get back to the Flag, I will think about that. Now, I believe the people I brought with me are beginning to rummage the brig. I had better go supervise while you examine the paperwork."

"Make sure you have a quill and ink handy. You will need to sign much paper before I leave."

"Sir", explained Phillips. "I must warn you, I had not realized we would be having visitors, when I put the ship out of discipline. The men and their women partners may seem a bit boisterous."

"Well, Captain Phillips, I rather thought there were more than a dozen people aboard. I may well need to ask some of your people to assist in moving gear around."

Alone, Tim began going through everything Captain Wilson had left. He found that he would be required to sign for literally thousands of items, the exact quantities blank for now. He assumed these would be filled in after the inventory.

Searching in the lockers, he was not able to find a pen or quill, although he did find a small horn container of ink powder. When he shouted for the ship's boy, William came running. The boy was older than his size indicated. Having spent his life on the docks, subsisting on whatever scraps he could locate, his body was stunted, but his wits were certainly sharp enough.

"William, I need a pen to sign some documents. Would you know where to locate some quills?"

This was a puzzler for the lad, but then an idea came to him. In the past, when he had been horribly hungry, a few times he had been forced to kill seagulls for food. They were most unsatisfactory provisions, but the larger birds might have feathers that suited.

Nodding his head, he said, "Yessir, it may take some time, but I think I can find something". Going forward, Will approached Bosun's Mate Rodgers who was supervising the men hauling the brig's sails from storage in the sail locker out on deck to be inventoried.

The petty officer listened to the boy,nodded impatiently and waved the lad off. "Don't be bothering me right now. Can't you see we have work to do here?"

Will ducked below, coming back up with a ball of light line and a fish hook. Baiting the hook with a scrap of cooked pork from dinner the day before, he set the scene by throwing a few other scraps of meat on deck.

One of the hands shouted at him to 'Belay', when he saw the boy throwing garbage on the clean deck, but was busy doing a task Rodgers had assigned and did not try to stop the lad.

Flocks of gulls wheeling over their heads swooped down to scavenge the meat. Will tossed the last few scraps on deck along with the baited hook and line. A big skua was hovering over the deck, trying to confiscate meat some of the other birds had secured. Seeing the new food thrown on deck, the bird grabbed the baited hook and attempted to fly off.

Will gave a tug on the line, setting the hook and drew the flapping pirate in. Before the big bird could do him injury, he bashed it with a belaying pin.

Rodgers appeared before him. "I know you did this for the Cap'n, lad, but you will clean up this mess you have made. Throw that bird over the side when you have what you want from it."

Will pulled the biggest feathers from the bird's wings, and threw the bloody carcass over the side.

CHAPTER TWO

Tim examined the quills wryly. These were not exactly like the type of goose quills one would purchase in a stationer's shop, but he imagined they would serve until he could find something better. He had already mixed some ink, and now trimmed the nibs on the quills with his pen knife, and tried one out. He decided it would serve.

Captain Wilson entered the cabin with a tall, cadaverous looking man. The man carried a short piece of board on which were pinned some papers. Wilson introduced the man as 'Jefferson, my clerk', and went to the stack of papers on Phillip's desk. He handed them one at a time to Jefferson, who marked figures on them furiously, apparently from memory, and handed them to Phillips.

He tried to read each as it was handed to him, but it was impossible at the speed the clerk was working, so he ended just by scrawling his name with the small pen and hoped he was not signing his life away.

At the end of the session, Wilson noted they had set a preliminary value on the brig which would be submitted to Admiral Cotton and the Admiralty.

Wilson commented, "You will note on that first page the clerk handed you, the brig's name is now 'Alert' Her signal number is also on the page, which you will need to give to your signal officer."

"Sir", Tim answered, "I have no signal officer. The only other person in authority aboard this brig is my bosun's mate."

"Yes, I must remember to send you some people when I get back. We are in rather a hurry here. While we wish you to have a full complement of people, we may have to wait until you make port again to completely fill your roster. I do realize we are sending you to sea in a hurry. Later on we will have to attend the details which we are passing over here."

"One complication arises from the unusual nature of your posting. Normally, of course the commander of a brig would be a lieutenant, with a more junior lieutenant under him as first officer. Then, there would be a senior master's mate to assist you with navigation, storing ship, and the like. Since you are a master's mate in command, we cannot put a commission officer in the brig as first officer, and likewise, a senior master's mate would not be wise, while a man junior to you would likely be worthless."

"We have hit upon a compromise. Since you will be sailing to the Baltic, you may need to have someone with a specialized knowledge of that area."

The captain excused himself and went out on deck. Returning momentarily, the flag captain introduced him to a short, round individual in a tattered blue coat. "Captain Phillips, I would like you to meet Captain Jensen. He is a Dane with a British mother, and speaks English perfectly. He has had disagreements with his country's leaders over the Danish alliance with Napoleon. Captain Jensen has agreed to accompany you to the Baltic to advise you as to conditions there."

"He is a merchant captain, as well as a Baltic pilot, and you may trust his local knowledge. He is, of course, a civilian employee of the Navy. He holds no warrant, and you remain responsible for the conduct of your mission, and the safety of your brig. You may use Captain Jensen's local knowledge of the Baltic area to safely complete your mission. He has a complete selection of charts for the Skagerrak-Kattegat waters you will be using to access the Baltic."

"Your orders have not been completely drawn up yet, but I'll send them, commissioning pendant and mail bags over in the boat with the additional crew members that you are allotted. You may keep the boat and its crew. I think you will find the boat better than the one you have now."

The launch as it came from HMS Intrepid the following day was a shabby vessel indeed, straight out of the dockyard's boat pond, devoid of paint but it was filled with seamen and their sea bags. A midshipman sat in the stern sheets with a sailcloth bundle. The seamen, mostly a glum lot, boarded the brig, and were handed off to Rodgers. The mid doffed his hat on boarding, and handed the packet to Tim.

"Sir, my name is Thomas Dale. I am instructed to inform you that your orders and ship's commission are in this packet. We could not get all of the crew in the launch, so I would like to send it back for the remainder. I am to tell you, unless you have questions, you are free to depart when wind and tide serve."

"Thomas Dale, just where in the scheme of things do you come in?"

The lad pulled out a folded parchment from under his jacket and handed it to Tim. Captain Phillips learned that Mister Dale was to report on board HMS Alert and assume the duties of a midshipman.

"How are your navigational skills, Mister Dale? Well, never mind, I'd rather be surprised! Every day at noon sights, you will be on the quarterdeck with me to tone your skills."

"Now, I see that you have brought me a number of new hands. Just what may I expect?"

"Sir, most are ordinary seamen, with a few landsmen. Captain Wilson sent you Harris, a landsman who can read and write. He said you may want to try him out as your clerk. Then, there is Davis, we think is a runaway apprentice. He might serve as your servant."

"You 'think' he is a runaway apprentice, or you 'know' that?"

"Mister Allison, our third officer on Intrepid thought he remembered him as a servant in the 'Bear and Bull Inn', but wasn't positive.

"That is well, Mister Dale. Since we don't know he is a runaway, we need not feel guilty for pirating him away. Right now, before we become involved with other matters, you had better fetch the remainder of the hands."

The original members of the crew were much disgruntled, having had their spell of 'Out of Discipline' cut short. It might be a trying time for the new members of the crew as they meshed with the old. Since there were many more of the new men, though, Phillips forecast the oldsters would need to temper their animosity.

With everyone aboard, Phillips called Dale aside. "Because you are to all intents and purposes the brig's first officer, I want you to go forward and enter all the new hands in the ship's books. Later, you and I will go over the watch and station bill to determine just where we will place each man"

That evening Captain Phillips pored over his orders. They were simple enough. He was to sail for the Baltic to deliver mail and dispatches to Admiral Saumarez. He was required to lend Admiral Saumarez such assistance as was required, and only after being released was to return to Portsmouth with whatever mail and dispatches he was provided. He was especially warned to avoid seeking combat with enemy ships, but was to defend his ship and his dispatches with all means at his disposal. If, at any time, it appeared his brig was about to be taken, he must dispose of all dispatches so they could not be captured.

The next morning wind and tide being suitable for departure, he ordered Dale to signal their readiness. In due course, the 'Proceed' signal was hung out, and HM Brig Alert won her anchor and set sail.

Both Phillips and Dale were extremely busy. It was necessary to train the men in both gunnery and sail drill. Tim's finances being what they were, he was not able to take a leaf from his father's book and purchase extra powder and shot for practice. However, the brig had been captured with a full load of ammunition issued by the French navy.

Captain Wilson had told him some of the brig's ammunition may have been 'overlooked' in the count, so he knew he had a fair amount to use for practice which he need not account for. The brig had received a full issue of ammunition from the dockyard, although there was grumbling about the need to locate French ball that would fit the enemy made guns.Wilson advised he would receive British issue nine pounder guns when the brig was at leisure.

Every day that was suitable, the guns left a pall of smoke to leeward from their practice, and every day the crew practiced their sail drill.

By the time they rounded the Skaw, and entered the Kattegat, Phillips could consider the brig ready to meet any enemy of their own size. There was plenty of concern navigating the Kattegat, especially at night when they entered, with its twisting channels. Phillips had learned to trust young Dale, and one or the other of them was constantly near a leadsman in the chains to keep themselves aware of the depth.

The first evidence of trouble the Alert had seen on her voyage came shortly after entering the Kattegat. Their lookouts had been seeing plenty of fishing boats, but following their orders, stayed clear of them. However, at dawn, a herring buss came out of the mist to windward of Alert. This was a large fishing vessel that was common enough to encounter, but this one had a few guns.

Apparently its owners had thought to try their hands at a little privateering. At any rate, though Alert gave way to the vessel, the stranger was having none of it. She fired a gun in front of the brig, pitching the ball right up under her bowsprit.

Visibility was poor that morning with fog and light rain, and probably the captain of the buss thought the plain looking brig was carrying cargo. Alert was a very beamy craft, with plain brown paint covering her hull. She was not what one thought of when one spoke of a King's ship.

Alert's commission pennant was flying, and she wore her red ensign, alerting all and sundry she was a British warship, and not some trader to be trifled with. Even so, the herring buss, after coming up on Alert's quarter, fired off her broadside of four little four pounder guns.

Alert had just cleared for action, as she did every morning at sea, and coming around a bit to port, run out her guns and fired off her portside eight pounders at the privateer. Alert carried fourteen of the French made guns, so seven of them replied to the pitiful two gun salute of the buss. Most of the balls hit, and did terrible damage to the converted fishing boat. The privateer had originally been designed to hold quantities of fish and was not intended as a warship able to withstand cannon shot.

As the gun crews went into their reload drill, the captain told Mister Dale to have the guns reloaded with canister. This was a metal can filled with small caliber shot. Upon firing, the can fell away at the muzzle, sending a cloud of small shot hurtling toward the enemy.

There was little of the canister on board, but every gun had a load, as well as grapeshot nearby, so changing the loads did not slow the loading tempo.

The enemy vessel was still shocked by the vehemence of the brig's reply to their challenge, and had not managed to get a gun ready to fire again. Her captain apparently was of the philosophy, 'Fire, and board in the smoke!' Her surprised crew had not expected the smashing broadside from what they had considered an under armed trader.

The former fishing vessel was crammed with every last man her captain was able to cram aboard. The privateer would not stay at sea for lengthy periods and did not need to carry large amounts of provisions.

Alert's guns fired again as soon as they were loaded, and the deck of the enemy was swept clean. There was now no sign of their colors, and no one upright on the quarterdeck. The privateer had been crowded with a mob of men serving as boarders. Many of these were down, and the deck of the buss looked like the floor of a slaughterhouse at the end of a busy day.

Phillips ordered his guns to cease fire, and the brig sat poised in the water, ready to resume fire should the enemy wish. Eventually, a junior officer on the buss waved a white flag, and the fight was finished.

Phillips sent Dale and his bosun's mate to inspect their capture. Neither was much impressed. Rodgers reported the capture was an aging fishing boat that had been given four small guns and sent privateering. Her hull was shattered, and Rodgers doubted she could make the voyage back home.

Accordingly, the few remaining survivors were taken aboard Alert, and the buss set afire.

CHAPTER THREE

Alert made her way into the Baltic, via the narrow passage between Helsingor on Danish Zealand, and Helsingborg on the Swedish coast. The batteries on Zealand were under French control, and would be dangerous if passed too closely. Phillips' instructions mentioned the confusion regarding Sweden's stand with the warring powers. Bonaparte was applying pressure on that country to deny access to British ships, and indeed to wage war on Britain. No one was quite prepared to say which way the nation would go.

The passage between the two countries being only a bit over two miles wide, Alert shaved the Swedish side to stay as far as possible from the known enemy Denmark. While batteries on Zeeland tried ranging shots, the Swedish batteries remained silent.

Glad to emerge from the shallow Kattegat, Alert encountered one of Admiral Saumerez' scouting frigates. Directed to the fleet's location, Alert saluted the flag in HMS Victory. The brig flew the signal, 'Have Dispatches' and was directed to fall into trail behind Victory.

Summoned to repair on board the flag, Phillips, already closely shaved, in his best coat and scraper, went over the side into the launch. The formerly plain, shabby boat issued them back in Portsmouth, had been titivated under Bosun's Mate Rodger's close scrutiny, and now was sparkling white, and would not embarrass the brig.

The boat crew had also made themselves clothing from the white duck fabric supplied by the clerk substituting for the non-existent purser. Altogether, brig, launch and crew presented a most professional picture to anyone watching from Victory's quarterdeck. As a mere master's mate, Phillips knew better than to board at the traditional starboard entry port, and ordered the cox'n to go around to the port side.

When challenged by Victory's watch officer, Phillips merely answered with an 'Aye".

Boarding without the aid of side boys or the stamp and clash of Royal Marines, Phillips was met by the curious watch officer.

He saluted the quarterdeck and the officer himself, then gestured to the crew in the boat to send up the mailbags. He already had the dispatch case attached to a lanyard around his neck. The lieutenant who greeted him wondered where the brig's commander was. Tim had to explain he was in command. Further questions had to wait, when an ill-tempered captain on the quarterdeck wondered what the delay was all about.

Hurrying aft, Phillips handed the dispatch case to the captain, while a pair of seamen lugged the mailbags aft. Impatiently the liner's captain waved the men with the mailbags to the first officer standing by, and asked Phillips, "You have dispatches for Sir James?"

"Yes sir." He said, handing the case to the captain.

"Follow me." He said, heading for the great cabin.

Sir James accepted the package with a smile, and cut the cords with a pen knife. Reading through some of the papers rapidly, he snorted at one and handed the paper to the flag captain.

Keeping his silence, as befitting a person that knew his place, Phillips stood there at attention. Saumarez looked at him, and wondered. "Where is your captain, Mister? I hope he is intact?"

"Sir, I command Alert. Admiral Cotton said I was too young to promote, so he gave me the command in lieu of promotion."

The flag captain chuckled, and said, "This is a new one on me, Sir James."

"Come on my boy, we get little gossip from home here. Tell us what you did to gain this command?"

"Sir, I was a mid on my father's frigate, when we captured the brig from the French near the mouth of the Tagus, off Portugal. My father, Captain Phillips, had already sent most of his officers away in other prizes and had no one he could spare to command her. He gave me a temporary posting as master's mate and ordered me to take command. Later, on the way south down the Portuguese coast, we encountered some French ships."

"My father engaged a forty gun frigate and defeated her. With the frigate was a schooner-corvette which my command engaged and took. Admiral Cotton confirmed my appointment as master's mate, and put me in command."

"I will be damned", mused the admiral. Raising his voice, he shouted for his servant. The servant, with an air of ill-use on his face, appeared.

"Bring a chair over for this young man to sit on, then get him some wine. Not that swill you try to serve me, but the good article that you and your mates drink from my stores!"

The indignant servant went off, bringing back a ragged looking chair. After he left again, Saumarez chuckled, "That man has been suffering since I took him as my servant back when I was a lieutenant. He knows the fleet would sink if it were not for his labors."

The wine was cool and refreshing. Phillips commented on it, and the admiral said, "I have a little basket that will hold a half dozen bottles. Jenkins puts it overboard on ten fathoms of light line. Some people do not know this, but the sea temperature generally gets colder the deeper you go. An hour at fifty fathoms here in the Baltic, will give a nice chill to our wine."

While Phillips finished his wine, he noticed the flag captain had left. "Captain Phillips, you will oblige me to take some papers of my own back to Admiralty. We also have some mailbags that I hope you will take back and put into the hands of the Post."

Looking at Phillips sternly, the admiral wondered. "Now then Captain Phillips, I see from your report that you had a little action in the Kattegat. Would you tell me about it?"

Phillips had put the details of his action in his report to the admiral, but now went through it again verbally. The admiral considered. "Very well, the buss was to windward close by when the mist cleared that morning. She fired at you. Was there no way you could have avoided her, if you wished?"

"Sir James, she fired as soon as we saw each other. She missed us, but I could not know if her gunnery was to continue to be so poor. Alert is not the fastest brig in the Navy, and had I ran, I considered that she could continue pounding us with those four pounders. I decided my best option would be to take her."

"No doubt you were right, Captain. One of my problems is, most of my officers are veritable fire eaters, who think a boarding action in the smoke is the proper action in most encounters with the enemy. The dispatches that you carry in your small craft are most important to the Navy, and it would be serious indeed if one of the bags were captured."

"You must always remember their safe delivery is the most important matter, even if you could be accused of showing the white feather in evading an action."

"I do note you burned your prize rather than attempt to bring her in. That shows common sense, which I value. Whenever I see a commander whose sole ambition seems to be taking prize after prize, to the exclusion of all else, I have to wonder whether he should be in command of one of His Majesty's ships of war."

"Well, Sir James, she was really only an old fishing boat with a few guns. We had beaten her up rather badly, and I didn't have enough men to repair and man her, as well as deliver my dispatches in a timely manner."

Admiral Saumarez nodded, and bent over his desk, scrawling something on a sheet of paper. Folding it, he held a stick of sealing wax over the flame of a candle and dripped wax on the note to close it. Pressing his own seal into the soft wax, he dropped the note into a mail bag beside his desk.

The flag lieutenant, standing inconspicuously behind the desk came forward and slipped a slotted piece of lead over the bag's draw-cord. The officer carried the mailbag over to the nine pounder gun in the admiral's office, and pulling the cord taut, he placed the lead seal on the gun's breach and pounded it closed with a little hammer. A steel stamp placed over the lead and pounded, sharply pressed the seal into the closure and ensured nobody could open the bag without notice.

Admiral Saumarez said, "I believe, Captain Phillips, that our business is concluded. If you take that mailbag with you, I would be glad if you would place it in the hands of the post in Portsmouth."

CHAPTER FOUR

Back aboard Alert, Phillips had Dale in his cabin, relating the subject of the talk the admiral had just given him. "I think it's a damned good thing we burned that privateer. Else, Sir James would be certain we youngsters were just whoring after prizes and to hell with our duty."

"Speaking of which", Phillips wondered, "what are we doing just sitting here?"

Pointing out the stern window, Dale said, "The flag has had a signal flying to the squadron, 'Send mail to Alert'. I thought we ought to wait until all the boats had reached us."

With the help of Captain Jensen, the brig slipped through the narrow waterway between Zealand and Sweden at night. Phillips had been informed back on Victory that Sweden was still neutral, but how long that might last was anybody's guess. By hugging shore, with the two boats ahead with sounding poles, Alert passed with little apparent notice. The crew of a fishing boat pulling their nets waved, but sounded no alert.

Proceeding northerly, remaining in the deeper channel, Alert's lookout spotted a sail off her port quarter. Phillips was not at first concerned since the passage between the Baltic and the North Sea was heavily travelled, mostly by peaceful merchantmen.

As this vessel neared, it was seen to be a brigantine of about their own size.

Under normal circumstances, she might have been investigated closely, but with the warnings he had received, Phillips ordered Alert to steer clear. Turning to starboard, the brigantine followed.

The stranger had Phillips attention now. He ordered Dale to loose the fore and main topsails. The activity brought Captain Jensen on deck. He had been nursing a streaming cold since they had left the fleet, but he was all business now. It would be to his benefit if he were not captured. Danish officials, should he it brought to their notice he had been assisting a British warship while in Danish waters, might well regard him as a traitor. He began taking bearings on landmarks to fix their exact position.

He reported there were shallows aplenty here, and he wished to take no chances of running aground.

The breeze had calmed, and there were fog patches up ahead. What wind there was came fitfully from the west. The brig was barely making steerage way. Jensen pointed to a tiny island on his chart. "That is Anholt, shoal water around it. We do not want to come too close to it. According to my reckoning, she should be dead ahead. Perhaps we should considering changing course?"

On Captain's Jensen's chart, he saw, just to the east of their marked course, the tiny island, right near the center of the deep channel. He asked Jensen just how sure he was of the ship's position. Jensen did not answer, but looked at him scornfully.

Calling Dale over, Phillips showed him the problem. "I want us to veer to port a point. We need to put some sharp eyes right up in the bow to warn us if we come too close. Warn the lookouts we are looking for land or shoal water."

Just before entering the fog bank. Phillips noticed the brigantine was still on their stern. As they entered, it seemed to be a different world. The wind was now just barely pushing them through the water. The only noise was from the lapping of the sea on their hull, and the creak of their rigging.

Moisture was condensing on solid surfaces, and Phillips sent the boy around to the guns to warn their crews to cover their priming quills. As they crept along in the silence, a warning came from aloft, *sotto voce*. "Deck there, land off the starboard bow!"

"Mister Dale", Phillips ordered. "Would you please jump up to the masthead and let me know what you see?"

While Dale was running up the rigging, Phillips ordered the helmsman to steer another point to port. As the brig slowly made its slight course correction, Dale came sliding down the backstay, and reported, "Land is on our starboard bow, a cable's length away. The fog is mostly lying low, and

I could see the hill tops on the island poking through."

Phillips went to the helmsman at the tiller. "Cooper, we have shoal water ahead and to starboard, with a privateer behind us. Do you think you can get us another point closer to the wind?"

"Yes sir, she is handling well."

The brig edged a little more to port. Not sure of his exact position, Phillips was cautious of making drastic course changes. The leadsman in the starboard main chains had been calling off the depths mechanically, but now Phillips realized the depths were increasing. Unless there was some underwater reef in their path, they might be safe.

On his own initiative, Dale climbed to the masthead again, and reported the island was now off their port beam, sliding aft. The fog was thinning to the north and west. It was still thick behind them, and Dale could see no sign of their pursuer. As Alert encountered a breeze that swept away the fog in their neighborhood, Dale announced, "Deck there. Enemy in sight on the starboard beam. She is south of Anholt Island, and is still in the fog bank. Just her tops are visible poking through the fog. If she has a man in her tops, he could probably see us."

"Very well, Mister Dale. We will change course back to the north."

The winds remained fitful for the next few hours. The enemy, on the other side of the island, had no way at present to get to them. As the wind increased and blew the fog away, no more was seen of the privateer. Alert made her way past the Skaw and out into the North Sea.

Alert came to anchor at Portsmouth, and Phillips was pulled ashore in the launch. The brig and her crew presented a more professional looking picture than when she had left. The boat had been cleaned, with the paintwork touched up. All the boat crew members wore matching jackets, trousers and sennit hats, all which had been made by themselves, or at least with the assistance of talented friends.

Phillips led a procession to the Port Admiral's shore office. Rodgers carried the dispatch package, the papers inside wrapped in tarred canvas, and tightly bound with light line. A pair of grapeshot inside ensured the package would sink in case it had to be jettisoned overboard to prevent capture

Four trusted hands trudged behind with the mailbags from the Baltic fleet. The flag secretary met them at the door, and sent a Royal Marine to fetch an officer to take charge of the mail. He himself confiscated the dispatch package and disappeared. Waiting, Phillips could imagine the consequences to himself should the secretary decide to desert to the enemy and flog the papers to Bonaparte.

All was well, though. The lieutenant appeared and led him in to the flag captain's office. Phillips was invited to sit down and give his opinion on some burgundy which had just come in on a prize.

After some innocuous discussion, Sir Roger Curtis, the port admiral came into the office and greeted Phillips by name. Tim had met the admiral before in company with his father, but had been certain the officer would not remember.

Sir Roger did, and asked if he had heard from his parent. When they finally got to the point, Sir Roger said, "Young man, in the dispatches you just brought from Admiral Saumarez, was one concerning yourself. In our service, you young commanders are expected to be fire-eaters, expected to always be champing at the bit to go out to capture another prize, or defeat an enemy ship superior to your own. Some officers though, especially those commanding dispatch vessels, are forbidden to do just that, for obvious reasons."

"Sometimes it is difficult for a superior to decide what to make of an officer that can follow the orders he has been given. One day to be a daring raider, the next as careful as a shopkeeper might be with his till."

"Admiral Saumarez told me about the privateer that attacked you near the Skaw. He mentioned you had burned the prize, rather than take men from your crew to send her home. He said that you deserved an independent cruise in your brig as a reward for your prudent behavior."

"In the report you supplied me of the voyage home, I learned of the incident with the brigantine in the Kattegat. Do you think you could have taken her had you engaged?"

"Yes sir. She was about our size, with the same number of gun ports. I do not know what weight of weapons she had, but my crew was well worked up, and I am sure we would have prevailed."

"Well Captain, I think I will do as Admiral Saumarez suggested. You will have your cruise. You will next report to Admiral Cotton; off Cadiz, at last report. However, I will not burden you with dispatches on your way there. The mail packet out of Falmouth will be sailing soon, and I will utilize her services this time."

"Take aboard what stores you will need, and you will then be free to depart. You may regard your voyage to the Iberian Peninsula a cruise, and may secure such prizes you may encounter. Furthermore, you will be sailing under Admiralty orders, so you may retain all three eighths of a prize's value, Goodbye and good luck, Captain Phillips. Good hunting on your way to Portugal."

The cruise to Spain elated Phillips, as well as the news about being under Admiralty orders. Normally, when a prize was captured, the captain would receive two eighths of its value, while the admiral commanding would receive one eighth. Under Admiralty orders, he would receive the extra share for himself.

CHAPTER FIVE

Along with the necessary stores brought aboard, some people came also. Another master's mate came aboard, to assist in navigation. Mister Henley was older than Phillips, and had been a master's mate longer.

Right away Henley decided to try Phillips on. Tim had greeted the new junior officer at the entry port, and invited him to his cabin for a drink, and to discuss the brig's operations on the trip to Spain. Since Henley had more service than Dale, he meant to use him as the brig's first officer, replacing Mister Dale. Henley started off on the wrong foot by addressing his captain by his last name. Then, he wondered how Phillips had been given the captaincy instead of himself, who had much more service.

Gaining confidence with every moment, Henley suggested that he might decide to visit the port admiral to see if he might wish to rectify the matter.

With his ire growing every second, Phillips decided he had remained silent long enough. Raising his voice, he shouted, "Pass the word for the first officer!"

"Mister Dale", he announced. "I have decided to appoint you master's mate. Mister Henley here, will revert to midshipman, to avoid any confusion over who commands this brig."

Henley sputtered. "You can't do this Phillips. I am your senior!"

"Henley, you may address me as 'Captain, or Sir. Anything else, I will deem insubordinate, and take the necessary steps."

"I'll see you damned, Phillips. I'll see the admiral over this."

"You will leave this brig immediately, Henley. As of this minute, you are dis-rated. You have no standing here now. You may wish to leave the brig before Mister Dale takes it into his head to press you as a common sailor. Mister Dale, would you get some seamen to help this civilian leave?"

Afterward, Dale approached Phillips on the quarterdeck. "You may have made an enemy there, Captain. If you lose this command, and he gets his rating again, you could be in for some trouble. By the way, am I still a master's mate now?"

"Yes, you are."

The summons was delivered by Sir Roger's flag lieutenant in the forenoon watch the next day. Lieutenant Henshaw was non-committal but reminded Phillips it was not wise to keep the admiral waiting. He left in the admiral's barge with Henshaw, after leaving instructions with Dale to send the brig's launch after him in half an hour.

Phillips cooled his heels in the waiting room for an hour. The admiral was not nearly so friendly on this visit, as he had been on the last.

The first question he had was, "What were you two schoolboys fighting about?" After a half hour of question and answer, the admiral's mood had lightened, and he called his servant in to bring them wine. No information was given to Phillips, and he left as bewildered as when he had arrived.

About ready to leave on the cruise down to Portugal, Phillips allowed Dale to go ashore to arrange for some wardroom provisions. On his return, he had news. From shore side gossip, he found Henley had, while in his cups, insisted on an interview with Sir Roger.

Uncharacteristically, the admiral did see him, and was assaulted with a barrage of demands that he, Henley, be given command of Alert, and Phillips be removed from the Navy.

Sir Roger had confirmed Henley's dis-rating and had him impressed as a seaman. Dale found later in his investigation that Henley was now serving aboard HMS Conqueror as a fore t'gallant yardman.

Dale thought, with Henley serving aboard a third-rate 74 gun, line-of-battle ship as an able seaman, it was unlikely he would get his midshipman's rating back soon, let alone be made master's mate. On a smaller ship, a shortage of officers who might be away on prizes, sick or injured, might cause someone like Henley to get his rating back. Not so on the big battle ship. It would likely have plenty of people in good standing with the captain who could be used as replacement officers.

The whole matter became moot on the day they sailed. The wind and tide were favorable, and Alert displayed the flag signal to request permission to depart.

The clearance was delayed, and Phillips thought he would lose the tide. Finally Lieutenant Henshaw came out in the admiral's barge and delivered a sealed document. Beside the officer in the barge, was a young midshipman, on his best behavior.

Opening the document, Phillips learned he was an acting lieutenant again, by Sir Roger's order. When questioned, Henshaw thought it was Sir Roger's idea to keep a similar event from occurring again.

Of course, an acting lieutenancy really meant nothing in the scheme of things. It could be taken away at a moment's notice. However, the acting commission would probably prevent another overly ambitious master's mate from upsetting the status quo and wasting the time of senior officers with more important matters to attens to.

Dale's appointment as master's mate was also confirmed, and Phillips was permitted to take on another midshipman. Normally, he would have been able to select a young gentleman himself. Due to their imminent departure though, Sir Roger had simply ordered a member of his flag's gunroom to jump down into the boat.

Phillips also found he was authorized to take on both an assistant surgeon, as well as a sail maker also, although where he was supposed to find either was a mystery.

CHAPTER SIX

Alert finally put to sea on the last of the ebb, and made her way out into the Channel. Crossing over to sail along the French coast, she was asked her business by a young frigate captain then indignantly told to remove herself from the area. This was apparently the Channel Fleet's private hunting preserve. Sailing south down the coast to the Spanish Peninsula, she was more welcome, but very little shipping was present. Finally, nearing the Portuguese coast, while running inshore at night, Alert's deck lookouts spotted something silhouetted against the lights of a military encampment on shore.

Phillips had planned on bombarding the troops, if he could escape much damage from any shore battery that might be present. The object appeared to be some kind of ship at anchor, so sending out Mister Dale in the launch, and Mister Rodgers in the cutter with their boarding parties, Phillips waited to see what the dawn would bring.

With no interference from the troops ashore, the trabacollo came sailing up to Alert, with the boarding parties aboard, and the boats towing behind. Dale's report related how the men swarmed aboard at the bow and the stern from the boats. There were only a pair of watch standers on deck, and they were overpowered without a shot being fired.

The rest of the vessel's small crew were told to stay below deck, and they followed their orders. An examination of the ship produced her manifests, and she proved to be the French flagged ship Adelaide with a cargo of flour and rice.

Trabacollos were generally considered Mediterranean craft not usually found outside the Straits, but Phillips heard France had taken some Venetian craft when Bonaparte siezed that Republic, and many of them were brought to Atlantic ports. Whatever her history, Alert's captain was sure the prize money would be useful indeed.

The trabacollo had just been sent off with its prize crew, under the command of Bosun's Mate Rodgers, when sailing past a small cove defended by a battery, they saw a schooner anchored close to shore. Phillips would have liked to emulate his father's practice of landing a force on the shore, then taking the battery from behind and confiscating any craft in port.

The crew of Alert was rather small for such activities though, so sailing on, as if giving up on the idea, she sailed back far out to sea where shore lookouts could not see her. Approaching the shore on the next night, she again loaded her boats with seamen and launched the raid. Since Dale had led the previous raid, Phillips led this one.

Rather than attempting to take the battery, he thought he might attempt to stealthily take the schooner by herself.

With muffled oars, the boats crept slowly toward their prey. The men had all discussed the amounts they would likely get when prize money came their way, and they were enthusiastic about earning more. The schooner was not as quiet as the trabacollo had been. There was a party of some sort going on in the after cabin, with plenty of noise.

The launch Phillips was using crept under the stern of the schooner. Bending the painter to a rudder pintle, one of the surer footed hands climbed the hull, dropping a line to the boat below. Edgars, a powerful looking sail maker's mate pulled himself up, then Phillips followed.

Edgars had an axe slung on his back, while Phillips had the wickedly sharp sword his father had given him, as well as two pistols in his sash.

When ready, Edgars smashed the glass of the stern windows, and pulled himself inside with the accompanying screams of women, and the roars of outraged men. Phillips looked inside, and watched a slim dandy begin to advance on Edgars with what looked like a court sword.

Holding on with one hand, he held his pistol in the general direction with the other, and fired. The heavy ball took the man in the lower leg, and dropped him to the floor. Phillips pulled himself inside into the turmoil, and fired his remaining weapon, to what effect he never knew.

More men were entering, and he heard a commotion on deck which told him the cutter's men had made it aboard. An elderly officer had engaged him with his sword, but Phillips quickly felt this man had not handled a blade in earnest in many years. A lunge to the shoulder brought both the weapon and the man to the floor.

There were women in the cabin, some of whom had apparent difficulty keeping their gowns covering their attributes. Having gone to sea at too young of an age to have been exposed to social events, Phillips was astonished at such behavior. One such woman, probably just a bit too old for such surroundings, had seized a carving knife from the table and was advancing on Phillips with deadly intent. The young man, flustered by the sight of what seemed to be acres of exposed flesh stood there in shock.

Peterson, a quartermaster's mate, and an old hand with the ladies, merely rapped her over the head with the flat of his cutlass, and stowed her in the corner out of the way. By now, the action had just about ended, although one woman considered it her duty to continue her highly pitched screaming.

Someone opened the door to a food pantry, and stuffed her inside, screams and all. The battery ashore had been woken by all the noise on the ship. The gunners were handicapped by the fact their two officers were both aboard the schooner, attending the party. The sergeant left in charge finally decided to fire when the schooner began to move, but not wanting to injure his officers, he made sure all the guns were aimed wide of the schooner.

Once out to sea, it was necessary to take stock. The schooner held a cargo of hides, as well as a quantity of sailcloth. Both articles as well as the schooner itself, would find a ready sale.The two artillery officers from the shore battery offered their parole, which was accepted. These officers would not serve in the French forces until properly exchanged for British captives of equal rank.

The captain and first officer of the schooner had both expired from wounds taken during the struggle. Others were civilians from shore that had been invited to the party. These were put in the boats and sent ashore with the women. The crew was interviewed, and it was found to be about equally divided between Spanish and French sailors. After the first officer explained to the prisoners of the likelihood of being sent to the hulks as prisoners of war, all the Spaniards accepted the option of taking service with the Royal Navy instead of going to the prison hulks.

The French were just as uniformly opposed to that idea. Phillips decided not to risk taking the obstreperous prisoners to Gibraltar in the limited space available and were allowed to crew the boats taking the civilians to shore. Alert and her latest prize made their way out to sea. With many of his crew gone into the prizes, Phillips did not wish to encounter any more enemy vessels.

CHAPTER SEVEN

Alert with her prize made port in Lisbon, and found she was not expected for another few weeks. The mail packet had come in with word from Portsmouth that Alert had been given a cruise. Admiral Collingwood was at sea with the fleet, but one of his frigates had just come in to take on fresh vegetables for the fleet's use.

As soon as Alert sailed into the harbor, and made her number, HMS Alceste hoisted the signal for Alert's captain to repair on board. Captain Murray Maxwell met Phillips at the entry port and took him into the great cabin. After finishing a glass of wine and exchanging the latest news, Captain Maxwell got to the point.

"Lieutenant Phillips, I was tasked by Admiral Cotton to come into port and take on what fresh provisions I could obtain for the fleet. Apparently the ships' surgeons have determined scurvy may be about ready to pounce."

"I have loaded aboard onions and lemons which I feel will fulfill my orders. However, I have since been approached by members of General Wellesley's staff who wish me to deliver urgent dispatches to Malta. If I leave on that mission, Admiral Collingwood's fleet may well suffer from the lack of the provisions I have gathered. Therefore, I am going to take you under my command and have your brig deliver the dispatches to Malta."

Phillips considered arguing with the captain, but realized it would serve no purpose. He had had his cruise, made a fair amount of money, and had to expect to go back to his work. He merely said, "Aye aye, sir", and waited for his instructions.

Captain Maxwell, relieved he did not have to ruin his digestion by arguing with the lieutenant, advised him to return to his brig, and await the dispatches from Army headquarters.

As long as they were parting on good terms, Phillips decided to ask for advice about his prizes.

"Sir, on the way down, I took two prizes. One, I sent to Gibraltar. The other is moored near my brig. Having never taken a prize before, I have no prize agent, and wonder what I should do about this."

"Well, Captain Phillips, my own agent has a representative here in Lisbon, as well as another in Gibraltar." He shouted for his clerk and told him to give Captain Phillips the name of the agent here.

"The Army will be all day getting the papers in order. I suggest you go ashore and see if Senhor Laveda can assist you."

Phillips had his boat leave him at the quay, and told it to return to the brig. He ordered Mister Akers, the new fourteen year old midshipman to alert the watch to keep their eyes open for him. He would wave his handkerchief from the quay when he wanted the boat to come back for him. That settled, he hired a boy to lead him to the place of business of Captain Maxwell's agent.

Trouble ensued when he tried to give instructions to the lad. The boy spoke no English, and the written address was a complete mystery to him. A priest walking by asked in good English if he could help. Phillips explained his desire to be taken to Senhor Laveda's office. The priest examined the note, and spoke in rapid Portuguese to the boy.

With a nod, the youngster agreed to the task, and held out his hand. At that internationally known demand, Phillips felt in his purse, and extracted a silver sixpence. With a yelp of joy, the boy ran ahead, only to stop and wait for Phillips. After being led through a bewildering maze of alleys, he found himself in front of a small shop. A brass plate set into the masonry announced this was the place of business of Senhor Laveda.

Phillips guide scampered off, and for want of anything else to do, he experimentally tugged on a braided cord that hung out of an aperture. A muted bell sounded inside, and a slightly built woman answered the door. When her burst of rapid Portuguese did not elicit any response from her visitor, she held up her finger, and left for a moment.

A young Englishman, dressed fashionably, came to the door, and stated. "Sir, I am Amos Drew, an associate here. May I help you?"

Phillips told the young man his problem and wondered if he could see a prize agent. Drew explained. "My uncle is the chief officer of our office in London. He has sent me here to learn the differing business practices here in Lisbon. The Laveda agency is allied with my uncle's office, and we can take care of your difficulty."

Informing Drew of the prize trabacollo in Gibraltar, the fellow dismissed his concern. "My uncle is associated with another agent there who will handle your business."

Drew informed him, after taking his particulars, the agency would see to both vessels through the different prize courts, and handle any legal difficulties that might crop up. When the vessels were condemned, they with their cargoes, would be sold at auction, and all monies deposited with his banker.

Phillips admitted he had no banker. Drew waved this off as a matter of no importance. "We can hold your funds until you do select a banker. For your information, a local banker here does have a relationship with Coutts where you may discuss opening an account."

With his immediate business taken care of, young Phillips decided to return to the brig. The prize agent could safeguard his funds until he was able to talk to a banker.

Knowing his guide was gone, Phillips asked Drew how he must go to get back to the waterfront. Drew took him out the front door of the agency and pointed down the street. "Turn left at the next cross street, and you will see the bay in front of you."

In the event, he was only a cable's length away from the quay where he had landed. He pulled out his handkerchief and waved it tentatively. With no sign of any activity aboard Alert, he held it up and waved it more forcefully. This time, after a few moments delay, he saw the ship's colors dip slightly, then the boat crew tumbling down into the launch.

On board, Dale showed him the bag of dispatches and gave him the written instructions which had been brought aboard while he was ashore. With everything understood, and a land breeze that would just take them out, Alert hoisted the signal requesting permission to depart. When no answer came after half a glass, Dale said, "I wonder if those Army people even know how to answer you?"

When the final grains of sand ran from the half hour glass by the binnacle, Phillips said, "To hell with them, let us up anchor and get to sea while we can. If they have any complaints, they can bring them to Admiral Cotton."

The crew now well versed in winning their anchor, the brig soon had the breeze on her quarter and was making her way to sea. As they left, signal flags rose to the signal mast on shore. Dale approached his captain with a frown on his face. "That signal they just sent is complete gibberish. Some soldier probably just pulled flags out of a drawer at random and ran them up the mast."

"Well, just send them a 'Not understood' and bid them goodbye."

More gibberish mounted the shore side mast, until it dropped out of sight.

With his orders, Alert could have just sailed through the Straits and on to Malta, but Phillips thought a dispatch vessel, such as Alert, might have an excuse to stop at Gibraltar. He did want to check on the disposition of his prize trabacollo, and hopefully retrieve his crew.

He entered harbor with no difficulties and took a boat ashore. A visit to the 'Convent', a former actual convent which had come into British hands a century ago at the conquest of Gibraltar, and now served as Government House, served no purpose. An official there did not deem it necessary for him to see the acting governor, but did find some military dispatches that needed to be sent to Malta.

Arranging for it to be delivered on board the brig, he went in search of the prize agent's office here. After some effort, he was led to the place by a pair of redcoats and went in to discuss his trabacollo. The letter from Lisbon had not arrived yet, so they knew nothing about him, but his papers which he had brought explained everything. Like the agent in Lisbon, the people agreed to handle his vessel through prize court and oversee the distribution of funds. He was told he really should visit a banker and obtain an account to which money could be remitted.

At their direction, he found the office occupied by a representative of Coutts and arranged for an account to which money might be sent. When he returned to the brig, it was already in the hands of the prize court and the trabacollo prize crew already aboard.

As Alert was preparing to sail, a lugger came up to the port side and announced they had mail to be delivered to Malta. This was normal post, rather than military mail and Phillips thought it would have been pleasant had someone asked him earlier to accept such mail, however he realized as an acting lieutenant, he had absolutely minimal influence here, so his best option was to do as he was asked, before someone made it an order.

An official at the harbormaster's office had told him there were few French National ships that he needed to be concerned about these days in the Med, but many privateers, indeed. It seemed any fisherman with a rowboat and a punt gun was given a Letter of Marque these days so he could go privateering.

The official's advice was to make certain the privateer could see his force before they became engaged. Most of these people were careful not to endanger their own vessel unnecessarily. The truth of this showed itself early on, when another of the ubiquitous trabacollos showed itself with a bone in its teeth coming up from behind.

These craft were built for trade, not for raiding, and were not usually very fast. This one was no exception, but she was just slightly faster than Alert. The brig had not been flying her red ensign or commission pennant, since both were becoming tattered.

However, now was the time to hoist them. The trabacollo was not impressed and fired off a six pounder bow chaser as she was closing. Unable to escape, Alert fetched to, and ran out her guns. A sensible captain might have called it a day and left for other pastures, but this one was stubborn and kept coming.

Alert's gunners were by now well trained. Every port side gun captain had his arm raised, indicating he was ready to fire. Phillips nodded to Dale, and he ordered, "As your guns bear, you may fire."

One after another, each gun fired deliberately. They were at long gun range, and the first few balls put up splashed near the oncoming privateer. Then, one hit the sea just short of the trabacollo and ricocheted into its hull. Then others found the range and began hitting the enemy solidly.

The vessel, unprepared for the assault, tried to tack, but her foremast came down as she tried to come about. Dale gave her a parting salute before Alert got before the wind again and sailed away.

Dale oversaw getting the guns housed before reporting to Phillips on the quarterdeck. "I wager that fellow will think twice before he tries to attack a British warship again. I wonder what possessed him."

Phillips advised. "To him we probably looked like an unarmed trading brig at first. Even after we showed him our teeth, he likely assumed the guns were quakers." Some merchant ship captains used black painted logs on their decks to simulate guns.

"We did some expensive damage to his brig. He will need a new foremast, and his owners will not be happy about that. Shouldn't we go back and finish him off? We could stand off and hammer him until he hauls down his flag."

"I think not, Master Dale. Admiralty will not be happy if we interrupt our voyage to take a prize. At the moment, we have merely defended ourselves. Anything further we do may incur their lordships displeasure. Besides, the vessel is already a wreck. If we had to pound her more, we might never be able to get her to port."

With the brig ready to run out her guns at the approach of any enemy, she made it to Valetta harbor in Malta without further incident. She unloaded her mail bags and the dispatch case without more such coming back on board. Phillips learned the scheduled mail packet had departed just the day before, clearing the postal office of all mail waiting shipment.

With no further orders awaiting, the brig cleared port and turned north, sailing around Sicily toward the Italian peninsula. Cruising up the western coast, she began to encounter coastal shipping. She stopped several traders and inspected their cargoes. A vessel carrying anything that could be construed as useful to the French military was burned, and the crews shifted into their own boats.

There was unrest in the brig as the men saw that potential prize money burn merrily away. Captain Philips tried to explain to the crew the impracticality of sending every small craft away with a prize crew, but few made much of an attempt to understand.

Alert did gain a few seamen as some of the Italian sailors voluntarily asked to join the ship. The reason usually given was their probable conscription into Napoleon's army when they reached a French controlled port.

With more men aboard than when they left Portsmouth, Phillips began actively looking for a vessel worth sending home. He found what he was looking for as the brig rounded Elba, between Corsica and the Italian mainland. She was a brig, much the same size as their own vessel, heavily laden and low in the water.

Flying the tricolor, Alert approached the oncoming brig as if she too, was merely rounding the island in a northerly direction to windward of the trader. When the two brigs were passing, Phillips ordered his starboard guns run out, and the ensign and commission pennant hoisted.

A forward gun firing told the stranger this was no mistake, and she immediately let fly her sheets, wallowing to a stop. Visiting the brig with the launch's crew and a boat load of men, Dale returned with a smile on his face.

"She has a cargo of wine in casks, as well as a large consignment of salt beef. The casks all have French military markings. Her captain and first mate are French, and she sailed from Toulon bound for occupied Cagliari on Sardinia. She is a good prize, Captain."

Many of the brig's crew were Italians, subject to conscription by the French. These men mostly volunteered to join the Royal Navy, believing this would be better than being a foot soldier in Napoleon's forces or rotting in the prison hulks. Dale stowed them below decks in Alert, picking out trustworthy crewmen from Alert to crew the prize brig.

With limited space to stow more prisoners, Phillips decided to sail for Gibraltar to drop off his prisoners and the prize. Then, he thought, it would be best if he returned to Admiral Cotton's fleet. His orders to deliver dispatches to Malta covered his absence, but now he felt he it was time to check in with the Admiral.

A suspicious senior office might very well surmise Phillips had been wandering the Mediterraneab lining his pockets rather than tending to the King's business.

CHAPTER EIGHT

Approaching the blockading fleet off Cadiz, the masthead lookout spotted the ships exercising. which included the flagship for Vice Admiral Sir Charles Cotton. Making her number to the flag, Alert was ordered to come under the three decker's lee.

Wishing he had a sailing master aboard with more experience than himself, Phillips maneuvered the brig through the fleet, and perhaps by accident,Alert found herself in the proper position without disgracing herself.

After a few moments delay, a flag hoist ordered Alert's captain aboard the ship-of-the-line. Phillips had become accustomed to the big Atlantic swells on the way from Gibraltar, but now, in the cutter, they seemed monstrous.

Determined to board the flag without making a spectacle of himself, he gathered himself as the bow man hooked on to the big ship. Waiting for his moment, he stood as the boat was rising on a swell, and simultaneously grasped the man ropes, and put his foot on a batten on the flag's hull.

The boat then dropped into the trough, leaving him stranded on the liner's hull. Before he could find the batten with his other foot, it had sunk into the water, soaking his foot and calf in the ice cold water. Getting himself together, he began the climb up the hull.

The flag captain met him at the entry port, and commiserated with him on his wet foot. Ushered immediately into the great cabin, Vice Admiral Cotton immediately asked him to sit and ordered his servant to fetch a towel. After the worst of the water had been swabbed off, Sir Richard ordered, "Captain Phillips, you must know that dousing your body in cold water as you just did is the best way to bring on the ague that I know. There is only one sure remedy."

Sir Richard ordered his servant to bring his own elixir for the prevention of ague. He disclosed the recipe to Phillips. "Patterson will take two measures of Navy rum, another of brandy and add that to a glass of Bordeaux wine. A raw egg is dropped in, and finally a quantity of crushed Jamaica pepper and Peruvian bark added. The medicine must be downed in one draught, or it will not be effective."

The servant brought a tall class nearly filled with the concoction and Admiral Cotton bade Phillips to down it in one gulp. Phillips needed to have several gulps, with the vice admiral urging him on. When finished, the combination of the spirits and the pepper left him barely able to breathe.

His superiors left him alone in the great cabin to recuperate while they went on deck to discuss matters away from his groaning.

When they returned, he had almost decided he might live. Sweating profusely, he listened to the fleet commander as he expressed his desires.

"I have read the note Sir Roger sent me concerning yourself from Portsmouth. He believes, in spite of your youth, you should receive the King's commission. I do not normally believe in advancing young men as young as yourself, but you have been resourceful and successful. Therefore, I have directed those captains present in my fleet to come aboard, and we will convene a board to examine your qualifications to become a commission officer."

Phillips tried to demur, saying that he needed time to study for the examination.

Sir Charles retorted, "Young man, you are either capable of commanding a King's ship, or you are not. If you are unable to convince my captains of your abilities, then you have no business commanding Alert."

When the board convened in the flag ship's great cabin, a half dozen midshipmen and master's mates were found to take it with Phillips. In light of his command of his own vessel, he was the first to be called. He was asked a myriad of questions concerning various naval subjects, some of them very pertinent, a few other concerned theories from ages past.

Sweating as heavily as he had when he had downed the admiral's potion, he stumbled through the examination, sure that he had failed.

After the individual board members put their heads together, the junior captain approached, held out his hand, and congratulated him on his passing. The flag captain came to him and informed him Alert would be dispatched to Gibraltar soon to deliver mail and obtain fresh stores for the fleet. "You will have a chance to post a letter to your father about your good fortune."

CHAPTER NINE

At Gibraltar, cattle obtained from across the Strait were loaded aboard. These were thin beasts, with little flesh covering their bones. Bosun's Mate Rodgers was highly incensed over the filth his seamen needed to constantly remove. Mister Dale, having no one else to assign the task of overseeing the cattle's needs, put young Midshipman Akers to the task.

Additional cargo was brought aboard. Bushels of onions, which, for want of another place to stow them, were carried in the ship's boats. Lieutenant Phillips contacted his banker's agent at Gibraltar, and found the prize he had left at Lisbon had already been adjudicated and the funds deposited to his account. The agent advised the Portuguese prize courts seemed to work faster than others he had known, and it might be wise to consider sending prizes there when possible.

Flush with funds now, Phillips ordered his crew to raise anchor, and the floating barnyard was headed out to sea, and back to the fleet.

Alert had almost managed to get the stink of the cattle scrubbed from her, when he was called to the flagship to receive dispatches he was to deliver to the blockading fleet at Toulon. It would be necessary to retrace their steps and pass through the Straits and up the coast past Spain to the French coast.

He was advised, while his dispatches were indeed important, there would be no barrier to his harassing French commerce or naval vessels on the way. It was considered important to disrupt the enemy's communications by sea as much as possible.

Phillips intended to be very careful about approaching any French naval vessels. While there were few French frigates or larger loose in the Med these days, there were any number of naval corvettes and smaller craft, some of which would be more than a match for Alert. The brig had never been a fast vessel, and she never would be. She was designed to hold stores capable of lasting months at sea, as well as guns and enough men to sail and fight her. She was not intended to win races.

Although poking into the small harbors they came to down the Spanish coast, and past Gibraltar, they found nothing until the lookout spotted a sail off Malaga. Young Mister Akers was thought to have the best eyes in the brig, so Dale sent him to the maintop with Phillip's good glass to spy her out.

Akers reported with a note of disgust that it was 'only a polacre'. The brig ran her down with as much dispatch as she could gather. Eventually, the strange looking craft heaved to and waited for the boat. Dale, with one of his Italian crewmen went aboard and found she was indeed an Italian vessel, sailing from Sicily bound for Toulon. Her manifest was brought aboard the brig and was examined by Phillips with the Italian seaman translating for him.

The vessel's cargo was raw sulphur, a necessary ingredient for the manufacture of gunpowder. This would be a welcome commodity back home. Bosun's Mate Rodgers, now used to captaining Alert's prizes was put in charge and ordered to take her in to Gibraltar. Phillips thought about sending her on to Lisbon, but was unsure how far Rodger's expertise concerning navigation extended. The prize court in Gib might not be as speedy as that in Lisbon, but he felt there was a better chance for the polacre to make Gibraltar.

Making her way to Cape Sicie, Alert found one of Admiral Collingwood's frigates that was keeping a close eye on Toulon. From her, she took a departure for the flag, and found her at sea exercising with the fleet.

Mister Dale took the dispatches and mail over in the launch, and received new bags intended for the Channel Fleet, then it was homeward bound.

After passing through the Straits and sailing up the Iberian coast, they met a much battered British sloop, HMS Amethyst, Captain Forrest.

Alert was flying the signal for 'Carrying Dispatches', but Amethyst displayed 'Require Assistance', so Phillips brought Alert to and sent the launch over with Mister Dale. On his return, he reported the frigate had been in action with a French line-of-battle ship, and had been badly battered. Captain Forrest being wounded but still in command.

Men were required, skilled seamen especially. The frigate had many casualties, and damage aboard the ship was extensive. Amethyst requested a carpenter's crew to assist with repairs to the frigate. Phillips went aboard with Alert's carpenter to assess the damage himself.

Captain Forrest had been badly wounded in a leg with a musket ball, and an oak splinter had punctured his arm. The frigate's surgeon had the officer wrapped up like a mummy, lying on a layer of hammocks on the quarterdeck, still in command.

His first officer was dead, and the second was badly wounded also. Phillips sent the boat back for more seamen to assist in repairs, and offered his first officer to assist the frigate's remaining officers.

Captain Forrest thought the carpenter and his crew were all that was necessary. He advised Phillips that his destination was the Bay of Biscay, off the Charente River estuary. He was to join the blockade of some French liners who had been penned up there by units of the Channel Fleet. Forrest thought he could get needed assistance and repairs there.

Phillips was not so sure. Amethyst was rather knocked about, with important members of the crew disabled. In his own opinion, he thought it would be better if the frigate returned to Gibraltar. However, he was only a lieutenant in command of a brig, and his opinion was not worth much.

Passing La Coruña, the pair entered the Bay of Biscay making their course north east. They .spoke HMS Pallas near Rochefort who told them the flag was off the anchorage of Basque Roads.

Admiral Lord Gambier saw Captain Forrest, who had to be pulled over to the flagship strapped to a carrying board lashed athwart his gig. Midshipman Akers delivered the dispatches but Phillips was not asked to appear until the next day. He learned, while Forrest had received plaudits for the defense of his frigate, Lord Gambier had not deemed him fit to continue in command because of his injuries, and ordered him back to Britain for necessary medical care.

Amethyst herself was given to a young commander out of a sloop, who now became a post captain. Phillips was anxious to turn over his dispatches, so he could resume his voyage back home. The voyage home was not to be, however, at least right then.

The transport ship carrying the wounded Forrest could also carry the dispatches. Alert would be needed here. When he did get to meet Lord Gambier, he was questioned closely about his religious views, and was told his brig would be assigned to the blockading fleet for a time.

His livestock and provisions he had loaded aboard earlier were now parceled out and distributed to the fleet under the supervision of an officer sent by Admiral Gambier.

CHAPTER TEN

HMS Amethyst had her crew reinforced and dispatched to Gibraltar under her new captain for repairs. Alert got her carpenter and most of his crew back. After a few days patrolling the seaward approaches to the Roads, Alert was called back to the fleet. On board the huge first rate Caledonia, he received orders to report to Captain Cochrane commanding HMS Impérieuse, who had taken station closer to the enemy ships he was monitoring.

Cochrane was an affable, capable appearing officer who called him aboard his frigate. There, he learned something of what that frigate captain had in mind.

Cochrane began. "A French fleet was driven into this anchorage earlier this year by ships of the Channel Fleet. Some French ships of the line escaped from Brest during a storm that drove off the blockading fleet. Their Admiral Willaumez then joined with more ships escaping from Lorient. They were driven into Basque Roads where they have been penned up since."

"You have met Admiral Lord Gambier already. He commands this fleet, of course. The Admiralty is concerned the enemy fleet may escape and stir up mischief elsewhere. I have been tasked by the First Lord of the Admiralty to destroy this enemy fleet by whatever means. I intend to do just that."

"Pardon me, Captain Cochrane. I seem to be missing something. Should not Admiral Gambier be giving me this information?"

"Aye, there is the rub, Captain Phillips. It seems that the Admiral is content to simply blockade the enemy, to prevent them from getting to sea. Their Lordships at the Admiralty, on the other hand, want them destroyed, so they may not haunt us in the future."

"The First Lord, Lord Mulgrave, asked me if I thought a fireship attack might be successful. I did, and have submitted a plan to send in fire and explosion ships, manned by volunteers and myself to see what we may accomplish. I was ordered by the Lords to attempt just such an attack, under the supervision of Lord Gambier."

"Admiral Lord Gambier is a fervent Methodist though, who disagrees strongly with the fireship plan, feeling that is not a Christian means of destroying the enemy. He may wish to prevent our success if he can."

"But sir, if there are orders from Admiralty to use fireships, I fail to see how he can prevent it."

"Captain Phillips, you are a young officer in command of a brig. I am a frigate captain. Admiral Gambier commands this fleet and is a former Lord of the Admiralty. With a seat in Parliament and many influential friends there, as well as in the Navy, he moves in circles much more elevated than the likes of us. He has much more leeway regarding orders than you or I do."

"The fact remains, I have my instructions from on high, and I will do my best to obey them. As for you, the good admiral has placed you under my orders, and no blame should come to you in regard to any disagreement between myself and Lord Gambier."

"For now, I want you to remain as close to the French ships at anchor as you can be, without taking undue risks. I will soon be taking HMS Impérieuse out to the offshore fleet for any last minute instructions that Lord Gambier cares to give me. You will signal the fleet, via the repeating frigates, of any movement of the French. Are you clear?"

"Yes Sir."

Alert patrolled just outside the enemy anchorage. One of the French frigates seemed to be preparing to put to sea. She was exercising her crew in sail drill, as much as she could at anchor, of course. When Mister Dale reported the activity to Captain Phillips, he ordered the alert signal hung out. The big liners were out of sight to seaward, but a frigate close enough to see the signal repeated it to the ships in the rear. A squadron broke away from the main fleet and approached the threat,

The frigate that caused the alert then stepped down, and the tension eased.

Occasionally, one of the enemy ships saluted Alert with a gun, just to see if the brig had wandered within range. Several enemy ships did have the range, but missed. After a few near misses, Alert moved out a few cable lengths, and all seemed well.

While this was going on, the master had the lead going, checking the accuracy of their charts. At night, when the enemy gunners could not see them, he took the launch inshore to get the depths closer in. This was difficult, since vision was limited. He had a dark lantern in the boat, and with the fitful light from this and his sextant, he took bearings from known lights on shore and enemy ships in the anchorage.

When HMS Impérieuse returned from the fleet, Cochrane conferred with the officers of the Inshore Fleet, asking for volunteers to man the fire and explosion vessels. Both Phillips and his first officer, Mister Dale, volunteered their services to command explosion vessels. After Cochrane's clerk had listed every volunteer, Cochrane called Phillips away from the others.

"Tell me about your first officer, Captain. Is he capable of handling your brig, and can he be relied upon to follow orders?"

"Yes to both questions, Captain."

"Very well, I will have the volunteers board Alert, and we will sail out to the fleet to collect the vessels we will use in the attack. They should be preparing right now, loading the powder and incendiaries. We will board our individual ships and return. You will be on an explosion ship with me, as my second in command, to take over should I fall."

"It will be your responsibility to see to the fusing of the incendiaries and gunpowder aboard our explosioin ship. You will have a means of ignition with you so there will be no wasted time finding fire when it becomes time to light the fuses."

"A floating log boom protects the anchorage, protecting the ships inside from attack. Our explosion ship will proceed toward the boom. When certain the ship will close it, we will ignite the fuses and escape in our boat."

"We will have only a few seamen with us. Your first officer will command Alert, and will accompany the explosion ship until coming one half mile before the boom. "

"A second explosion ship will be moored alongside Impérieuse, which will remain behind at a safe distance with some other frigates. I will use the second explosion ship as the occasion arises. These ships are former transports loaded with hundreds of barrels of gunpowder and other munitions. After we have the objective within reach, we will light the slow match and go over the side into our boat.

Hopefully, the explosion ship will continue on course until it fouls the boom and then explodes."

"Alert, with some other non-rated vessels nearby will take the crews on board, after we complete our mission. Should another explosion vessel be needed, I will return to our spare and take her in. With the boom out of the way, the fireships will then come through the gap we made and attack the enemy fleet at anchor."

CHAPTER ELEVEN

There was a strong wind that evening, with heavy seas. Caledonia's flag captain wondered if the attack should be postponed. Cochrane assured him that his people could still do their mission. There were two dozen vessels of various sorts to be manned and got under way.

A dozen transports were fitted out as fireships. They carried tar and pitch as well as all of the various ship's slush they could obtain. The slush was the congealed skimmings of the cooking pots after men's the beef and pork had been boiled. This, as well as the tar and pitch, when ignited, would burn furiously.

Gunpowder was judiciously spread around the ships. Some of it was meant to help to get the incendiary material burning quickly. Some containers were spread about the fireships intended to explode and spread fire to the intended targets.

In addition to the transports, three captured chasse marées, or 'tide chasers', already loaded with highly inflammable tar and resin were available, as were three explosion ships filled with barrels of gunpowder. Their decks covered with fused shells and grenades, would spew exploding shells and grenades upon any target within range when the main charges fired. A few bomb and some Congreve rocket vessels rounded out the inventory.

HMS Impérieuse was anchored at the edge of the Boyart Shoal. An explosion ship was made fast to her stern, in case Cochrane felt it might be needed. Near the HMS Impérieuse were anchored the frigates Aigle, Pallas and Unicorn, prepared to receive the boats of the fireship crews after they had finished their mission. HMS Caesar with the boats of the fleet, was also available to assist.

Once the crews were prepared, anchor cables were cut, and the various craft of the assault fleet began sailing toward the anchorage. Aboard the first explosion ship, Cochrane stood on the quarterdeck, judging the moment when the slow match should be lit. Phillips stood by with a dark lantern to provide a light. Should the flame inside the lantern be extinguished, he had two pistols in his sash that were primed but not loaded.

The wind was fair for the task, and the old transport seemed to be steady on course for the boom. The night was black as pitch, and they now had no sight at all of their target. Cochrane was navigating solely by dead reckoning. Knowing the distance to the target, and the approximate speed of their ship, he felt he could bring the ship right onto the barrier they intended to destroy.

Looking to port, Phillips could just make out the loom of Alert, with sometimes the faint glim of her binnacle light to give her a little substance. Towing behind Alert, he knew, was the launch, which the fireship crew hoped to find if something happened to their own boat.

Cochrane almost caught Phillips by surprise when he ordered him to start the ignition sequence. First, it was necessary to light the port fire which would be carried around to light the different lengths of slow match about the transport's deck. Phillips dropped down behind a bulwark to shelter himself from the wind. He cautiously pulled back the shutter of the dark lantern, and the flame promptly blew out.

All was not lost. He pulled out one of his pistols and held the port fire he wanted to ignite with his left hand. Ready to thrust it into the burning powder in the pan, he pulled back the cock, and pulled the trigger.

There was the usual commotion of a flintlock trying to fire, and this one almost did. There was an initial spurt of fire from the pan, which promptly died out. A bit of spray had probably dampened the priming.

A seaman saw his difficulty and handed him a wad of tow. From one of the bags of gunpowder on the deck, he obtained a handful of the deadly substance, and sprinkled it on the tow. Phillips laid the wad of fibrous material on the deck and held the second pistol over it and fired. Sparks from the pistol's pan fell on the tow, and it ignited in a furious flare. Thrusting the port fire into the flame that was ignited also. A second port fire was lit from the first, then Phillips went to work, lighting the various lengths of slow match that terminated at the quarterdeck.

Some of the slow match, judiciously cut to the proper length, led directly to the charges they were meant to ignite. Others, led to lengths of quick match that in turn were connected to more distant charges. The quick match burned extremely fast, a fathom would flash from end to end at the speed of an eye blink. The various charges were calculated to explode nearly simultaneously.

The first charge to explode would likely fire the rest immediately, but to eliminate possible problems, each charge that was separate from the others had a length of match that would fire it if necessary.

The slow match was intended to burn for half a glass, giving them fifteen minutes to get away from the ship. The transport was sailing on her own now, with the wheel lashed. Alert had already dropped away to wait for her moment. One of the seamen had already pulled up the launch and the crew tumbled down into it, Cochrane being the last to leave the fireship. The men bent to the oars, to get away from the ship as quickly as possible.

They had barely left the lee of the transport though, when the vessel exploded. No one would know for sure what happened. Cochrane thought the match was defective. Phillips thought it more likely that perhaps the burning ember of the match had found some spilled powder on deck, flashing toward a charge with unintended speed. Whatever the reason, hundreds of barrels of gunpowder exploded, sending a myriad of shells and grenades into the air, which soon rained down on them.

Some of the force of the explosion went down, and more went laterally, sending a ragged column of water and debris high into the air. Down came the water, along with baulks of timber from the destroyed ship's frame as well as the munitions.

Although the bombs and grenades were fused, not all of the fuses had ignited during the explosion, so these did not explode. Of those that had ignited, some fell into the sea before the burning fuse reached its charge and some were thrown far enough way so that no one was killed by a close explosive burst. However, there were sufficient nearby explosions to keep the men from becoming bored.

Two bombs dropped close aboard. One fell only a fathom off to port. Either its fuse had not ignited or the shell submerged before the flame reached the charge. This one did not explode. The second one did have a lit fuse, and it did explode, an instant before it would have fallen in the water. A wave between the shell and the boat shielded them from most of the force of the explosion.

After the seamen regained control of the boat, it seemed half of the hands had some type of injury from the explosion, mostly from falling debris. Able Seaman Hendricks received a piece of iron casing from an exploding bomb that struck him in the rib cage. Hendricks was immobilized in the boat's bottom, and Phillips took his place at the oar.

There was some confusion at first. Visibility was nil in the low lying boat. Soon though, a sharp-eyed lookout in Alert's bow spotted their boat and came alongside. Gaining the deck of Alert, they could see the fires ignited on board the many fire ships as they moved through the now demolished barrier. Cochrane muttered to himself when it became obvious that many of the ships had been fired early, and were drifting off course. In the end, not a single one found its way into the French fleet.

Cochrane had succeeded with his own immediate mission, having destroyed the log boom which had been intended to prevent access to the inner anchorage. But the main effort of the attack had seemingly failed, with the fire ships being fired and abandoned early, then drifting off course.

Next morning however, a different picture emerged with the rising of the sun. While none of the target ships had been damaged by the fireships, it seemed the individual French captains had been unnerved by the explosion, and the sight of the oncoming fire-ships. The ships of the enemy fleet had cut their anchors, and some had made sail to escape the flaming vessels, apparently thinking these were also explosion vessels. Many of the ships either ran afoul of each other, or ran aground.

The morning's low tide left many stranded in the mud flats, laying on their beams, with their bottoms exposed for all to view.

Cochrane signaled his admiral that the enemy was exposed to attack and asked for assistance. Gambier hesitated for several days, while Cochrane did what he could himself, under fire from shore side batteries. His ship approached dangerously close in the shallows pumping balls into the exposed bottome.

Unless the enemy crews could make the shot holes watertight before the tide came in again, the rising waters would flood the interior of each ship, ensuring she remained on the bottom.

Finally Admiral Gambier sent a small force with HMS Theseus in to assist, but recalled the ships soon after before accomplishing much, despite the repeated requests from Cochrane to finish the task. He was furious about the failure to finish the task when it was possible. Cochrane felt a determined attack by major portions of the fleet would have destroyed the enemy.

In the end, five of the French fleet were destroyed, with many others badly damaged. There were recriminations, which Phillips was grateful to evade when Alert was ordered to return to Portsmouth with HMS Impérieuse. Cochrane later became seriously involved with the controversy against Admiral Gambier, which ended by adversely affected his own career. Luckily, Phillips was well away from the matter.

CHAPTER TWELVE

Lieutenant Phillips, captain of HM Brig Alert stepped down into the launch in Portsmouth Harbor. Under his arm he carried all the papers he thought he might need to produce for the port admiral. In the event though, he never saw that worthy.

An over-worked elderly lieutenant with a pronounced limp relieved him of the documents and informed him of his immediate future.

"Alert will be going into the dockyard", the officer informed him. "As a recent capture, she should have been surveyed before, but I gather there were reasons that did not happen. Her French guns will be replaced with British weapons. She will be emptied and her hull, spars and rigging examined. She will receive a new suit of sails as well as the proper provisions and equipment."

"It is expected this will take a month to complete, so you may as well go on leave until she is ready."

"What about my crew? I know I will lose some, but I hope I may keep some of my key people."

"Phillips, remember that you are a very new lieutenant commanding this brig. I would have expected you would be removed from her and placed in the wardroom of a liner. However, the Port Admiral says we should leave you on board."

"Admiral Curtis does not give your crew the same blessing though, so they will be treated the same as other ships entering the dockyard for an extended stay. They will be removed and sent to a receiving ship, where they will be available for draft for others ships needing men. When it becomes time for Alert to sail, she will be furnished with men from the same source.

"When you have found a place on shore to live, you will furnish the dockyard clerk your address so we may inform you when the brig is ready."

Needing a place to stay after his time at sea, he began looking for rooms. He found a rather seedy lodging house near the dockyard where he could stay for a reasonable rate. The first item on his agenda was to locate the office of his prize agent here in Portsmouth. From him he learned another of his prizes had been adjudicated, and he was now well financed.

With money in his pocket, he decided to buy some decent uniforms, since his old coat and breeches were becoming worn. Another item he wanted was a sword. His father had given him one he had captured, but he felt it was rather ornate for a lieutenant's weapon. It would do for dress purposes, but for cut and thrust on an enemy's deck he thought a plain, sturdy blade would be better.

Phillips spent most of the week with these tasks, and had taken delivery. Wearing his new togs, he stopped by a book seller to see what they had he might occupy himself with at sea on his next voyage.

While poring over a book, another officer approached. Glancing up, he saw the gold epaulettes of a captain. Considering a book seller's shop neutral territory, he muttered, "Good morning, Captain", and went back to his book. The captain wandered off to another portion of the shop, and Phillips forgot about the officer.

When he made his selections and went to pay for them, the captain was already at the counter with his own purchases. The captain turned to him, and said, "Pardon me, have we met before? My name is Mullins, and a friend of mine, Captain Phillips, has a son that looks remarkably like yourself."

For the life of him, Phillips could not recall the man, but he admitted his father was Captain John Phillips and his own name was Timothy Phillips. The captain greeted him effusively and insisted he accompany him to a nearby inn where they each ordered a brandy, and compared notes.

Mullins reminded Phillips he had served under Captain Phillips, Senior, as a midshipman and lieutenant. He wondered where the captain was at the moment.

"Sir, the last I saw of my father was over a year ago, here in Portsmouth. He was leaving for the

Channel Fleet and I was for the Baltic. Since then, our mail has not caught up."

"Well Lieutenant, I am very glad to have met you again. You were a child when I last saw you. Tell me, do you have a ship?"

"Yes sir, I command the brig Alert, but she is in the dockyard for the moment, and I am at liberty until she is released."

"You are fortunate indeed to have a command at your age. I myself am about due to sail, and some friends and family will be giving me a farewell party at the Bull and Bear Inn tomorrow evening. If you are at liberty, you would be most welcome. There will be some very decorative young women at the party, if that might interest you."

Phillips thought about the invitation the next day. He did not really fancy the idea of attending a party attended by an old friend of his father, but on the other hand, the mention of the young women was interesting.

Having gone to sea early, he had not much experience with the gender, but was willing to learn. In the end, he donned his new clothing, belted on the ornate sword his father had given him and left for the party. Not knowing exactly where the inn was located, he engaged a cabriolet, and went there in style.

This event was not like the typical Navy party with free flowing rum and ribald song. The men were mainly over forty, and accompanied by their matronly wives.

However, there were some attractive young women there also, mostly squired by young Army subalterns and a few midshipmen from the fleet. He stood in the rear nursing a glass of wine while observing the others dancing. This was an exercise he had never learned, and was not about to embarrass himself by trying now.

There were others standing that were not dancing. A flock of juvenile mids were in the corner acting the fool, and a very attractive young woman, perhaps a little older than himself stood across the room. Phillips knew she would be busy soon, when the dance ended and those subalterns went looking for new partners.

He had finished his wine and was debating whether he could leave without offence, when he realized the woman was approaching. He hurriedly put his wine glass down, and gave her a little bow. She smiled and asked if he would get her a glass of wine.

Snagging a pair of glasses from a passing waiter, he gave one to the woman and began attempting small talk. He was distracted by her garb. She was dressed in a white lacy garment that was almost transparent in strategic places and left little to the imagination. One of the elderly men leered as he performed the introductions. Her name was Susanne Wilder.

She began questioning him about his parents and his naval service. His clothing was standard Royal Navy uniform, although it was evident it came from an expensive tailor. She was impressed by his sword which would have been an expensive purchase for the Frenchman who had originally commissioned it. Tim did not mention that his father had captured the thing in combat.

When she tried to interest him in the dancing, he had to explain to her that he had been at sea since boyhood, and had never had any instruction in that area.

She was thinking to herself that perhaps she had learned what she needed already; it might be time to set the hook. She murmured that she was feeling rather faint, and would like to go outside. Young Phillips offered to try to locate a physician or perhaps an older woman to help her, but she assured him she just needed some fresh air.

Outside the inn in the rear was a small lawn and garden, with seats scattered around on the freshly mowed grass. It was dusk now, and the light was fading fast. The seat she selected was separated from others, as well as the walkway by a tall shrub. Susanne thought the setting had possibilities.

Sometime later, Miss Wilder was wondering if she had made a mistake. She had asked some discrete questions concerning the young males at the dance, as she did at every such occasion. The subalterns were to a man, idle spendthrifts their parents had sent away to the Army to prevent them from selling the family silver to pay their gambling debts.

This young Phillips, according to Captain Mullins, who was very fascinated by her bodice, assured her young Timothy Phillips was a well off lad who commanded his own King's ship, and had made some prosperous captures. Miss Wilders was not knowledgeable about the Royal Navy's prize system, but another man present employed at the local Coutts branch informed her young Phillips had a most respectable balance, which she did understand.

The question was, how must she get the lad to take notice of her? He was aware of her charms, she could see him furtively looking every half minute. But he did nothing! Perhaps the problem was his age. She knew he would not be twenty for several more years yet, while she was about to turn thirty herself. With no dowry, if she was going to snare a husband, she was going to have to do it soon, before her looks started to fade. Young, healthy, rich males were not exactly plentiful in the circles she moved in.

Deciding to take the bull by the horns, she gave an emotional sigh and leaned back in the seat. Alarmed, young Phillips asked what he could for her. She told him in little gasps that she was feeling rather faint and could she hold his arm for a while.

"You are so strong!" she murmured, as she held his arm across her breasts. "That ought to wake him up", she thought to herself.

The young fool sat there rigid for a moment, then disengaged himself, got up, went into the inn and returned with Mrs. Harkins, an ancient biddy of over fifty. After Phillips discussed Miss Wilder's symptoms matters to her, she came over and questioned Susanne. She believed not a word Wilder told her, but told Phillips it was a simple female difficulty that would disappear soon. Sniffing and shaking her head, she strode firmly back into the inn.

Tim could have sat there forever gazing upon her, but soon the guests began leaving and Captain Mullins came over and told him it was time to go. Mullins debated whether he should warn the lad about Miss Wilder. Women of that sort were fine companions for temporary recreational purposes, but one must not marry them. In the end though, he decided the lad must learn his own lessons, as all men must.

The groom brought Mullin's carriage around and he gave the lad a ride to his boarding house.

Next day, his landlord brought him the post. In it was a notice from the dockyard that his brig would soon be ready to sail.

CHAPTER THIRTEEN

HM Brig Alert swung to her mooring in the morning sunlight. Smoke drifted from her galley chimney, but no other sign of human presence manifested itself from this distance. As the shore boat carrying Captain Phillips closed though, a short statured person appeared on the quarterdeck, a midshipman with a telescope under his arm. At his shouted, "Boat Ahoy!" the cox'n on the boat shouted, "Alert!"

There were a few people on board after all. He could see them running up from below. Before climbing aboard, Captain Phillips ordered the oarsmen of his hired boat to pull him around the brig. All in all, it was a remarkably well constructed craft. Others had warned him he would need to spend some money if he wanted especially fine workmanship from the dockyard.

He had crossed some palms with a bit of his prize money, and the expense proved worthwhile. The brig had been painted a rich brown, with the gun port lids painted bright yellow. A blue belt had been painted right around the hull just below those gun ports.

Those gun ports were filled with a pair of six pounder long guns at bow and stern, and ten thirty two pounder carronades in the broadside. The carronades were light weapons firing a massive ball with a reduced gunpowder charge. Phillips had little experience with the weapons, but was assured the guns could achieve smashing hits at a respectacle range in normal sea conditions.

Man ropes had been rigged, and he climbed up the side through the entry port. Two petty officers were serving as side boys, and the lieutenant he had met briefly the day before in the port admiral's office was there to greet him. He too, was not old enough to shave yet, but Lieutenant Walnright had a commission date a week after his own, and he appeared knowledgeable of his duties.

At this early date, only a few people that had reported aboard. The cook was present, as was the carpenter's mate who would be taking care of any problems with wooden equipment or hull repairs. He had been told Alert would have a sail maker on this voyage, as well as an assistant surgeon in the event anyone needed an arm or leg lopped off.

The crew would begin coming aboard this afternoon, soon after their detachment of Royal Marines reported aboard. There was a fly in the ointment. When Alert had arrived at the dockyard a month before, the crew that had been removed were mostly rated as either able or ordinary seamen. He had been warned the supply of such men was now very low, so many of the new crew members would be sweepings of the press.

Certainly, some of them would be skilled seamen pressed from merchantmen, but more would be itinerant farmworkers, runaway apprentices, criminals released from gaol and the like.

He did have a few midshipmen he could use as petty officers. It seemed every shopkeeper in Portsmouth had a son or nephew that wished to go to sea as an officer in training. With little room available, Phillips only accepted those young men who had already been to sea for a cruise or two, and could earn their keep. He wanted no ten year olds crying for their mothers on his brig.

That afternoon the remainder of his warrants came aboard, followed by a sergeant of Royal Marines with a corporal and a dozen privates. Shortly after, the boats began arriving ferrying out the new crewmembers. Some of the people were very strange indeed.

Phillips and Lieutenant Wainright set up a table and two chairs on the quarterdeck, where it was intended all new crewmen would pass by, give their names and a brief history of themselves and be entered in the ships books.

One of the first in the procession was a burly man in torn and filthy clothing with a wad of tobacco in his cheek. He was one of those released from gaol to enter the Royal Navy. He was sneering and contemptuous when he stood before his captain and first officer, but Phillips made no mention of his displeasure yet. He had decided to allow the men to become used to their surroundings before enforcing discipline. With no experience at sea, the man was rated as 'Landsman' and his brute strength would be used to pull on ropes and haul yards around.

After spending only a few minutes on the man, they handed him over to the midshipman who supervised the people in the waist of the ship.

As Phillips began to interview another man, he saw the big fellow spit tobacco juice across his deck, splattering the fourteen year old midshipman's feet. A bosun's mate had also noticed and went after the culprit with a knotted rope's end. Then there was a free for all on the quarterdeck. The big fellow took the rope's end away from the bosun's mate, and began punching the petty officer in the face with his fists.

A Marine got into the fray, but had his musket torn from his grasp and thrown over the side. The Marine sergeant and corporal then entered the conflict to show the privates how it was done. Each proceeded to smash the man in turn with musket butt strokes, pounding him 'till he was bleeding and senseless on the deck.

Phillips ordered Sergeant Reynolds to take the man below and secure him for the time being. There was muttering among the remaining members of the crew as they were formed up again before the captain and first officer to make their marks on the ship's book and receive their duty assignments.

Hoping there would be no immediate signals for him to report to the flag, Phillips summoned the Sergeant Reynolds before him after finishing processing the hands. Ordering the sergeant to report, Reynolds stood there at attention a moment, getting his thoughts in order.

"Sah, pris'ner is secured on the mess deck. Privates Atkins and Wilson watching him. Sah, there ain't no irons on the ship I could find, so we bound him up with line I got from the bosun."

"Very well, Sergeant, I'll see what I can do about the irons. Tell me, as the aggrieved party, what are your views about the disposition of this case?"

"Sah, can't say I understood some of them words you used."

"What do you think we should do with the prisoner? He deserves a court martial for striking you and the corporal. If I send him to shore, he will surely hang."

"Sah, if you please. You don't have to hang the man for me. If he tries us on again, my men will take care of him."

"Well Sergeant, unless you and the corporal press charges, I will bring the man to Mast on the charges of spitting on the deck, and contempt to officers. I assume he has been injured while resisting arrest. As soon as our surgeon comes aboard, I will ask him to examine the man to determine when he will be able to receive punishment. Thank you, Sergeant. Dismissed."

The brig was small, and sounds carried easily from bow to stern. Normally, there were plenty of shipboard noises to mask any particular sounds, but in a quiet moment, the captain thought he heard some muffled thuds, and a choked off scream. Absently, he hailed the Royal Marine sentry outside his door, and asked him if he had seen the first officer.

"Sah, first officer is on the quarterdeck, Sah!

"Would you pass the word for him please?"

While waiting, Phillips re-examined the inventory of shipboard items he had signed when he took command. When Wainright appeared, his captain waved him to the chair and asked. "Mister Wainright, I know we have no armorer on the books. Would you know if we have any man on board with that skill?"

Wainright thought a moment. "Sir, Landsman Warren is a runaway farrier's apprentice. He is the only one I can think of."

"Thank you Lieutenant. It seems we have no irons on board. I do notice we have a forge and a supply of coal for it. As a means of testing the man, perhaps you would have him set the forge up forward and have him attempt to make a set of irons, Better have some people standing by to make sure he does not set the ship on fire."

A glass later, Phillips became aware of the smell of recently lit charcoal and then the sounds of hot iron being beaten on an anvil. When he went on deck later, he found the new armorer hard at work beating out a bolt. A perfectly formed manacle lay in a bucket of seawater. The bosun's mate fished it out and showed it to the captain. It was a clever circlet of wrought iron, hinged so it could be opened. Two perforated clips extended out from the circlet. The bosun's mate explained a rivet would be passed through the holes, and pounded so it would not come out.

"Only way to get the irons off is for the armorer to drill the rivets out", he explained.

Phillips addressed the sweating man at the forge. "Warren, I admire your work. I have it in mind to appoint you ship's armorer. This will enable you to avoid being driven about from one task to another with the other landsmen. You will also be paid more. What do you think?"

"Sir, Your Honor, I'd be happy to be your armorer."

"Very well, Mister Warren, I will have you entered as such in our books immediately. Please go on with your work. We will need irons that will fit our current prisoner, and at least one other set to restrain a normally sized man."

Deciding to go below to inspect the prisoner, he was amazed to see his appearance. His face and exposed skin on his body was bloody and lacerated.

One eye was closed and the other open just a bit. His hands and feet were bound, with the feet also lashed to a stanchion. He glanced at the Marine guard and asked why the extra bonds.

The private answered, "Sah, Master at Arms, 'e comes by, an' 'Aynes 'ere kicks 'im."

"I see, Private. It appears Haynes has already received some punishment. Do you think he can understand me?"

"Sah, 'Aynes can 'ear well enough."

"Very well, we will give it a try. Haynes, when you put your mark on the ship's book, you became a member of His Majesty's Navy, subject to its rules. When you spat on the deck, you put yourself in danger of a dozen lashes. When you sneered at me, you put yourself in danger of a noose. When you struck the Marine sergeant and the corporal you again became subject to the death penalty."

"Haynes, I do not flog men on my ship any more than necessary. I would prefer not to send you ashore to a court martial to be hung. The sergeant tells me he does not insist on pressing charges himself. You should understand you put your life in your own hands whenever you show your contempt to your superiors. The private tells me you tried to kick the Master at Arms. He is another man who can have you hung. Do you want to have your neck stretched?"

The prisoner turned his head to Phillips and spat a bloody wad of spittle at him, missing his boot by an inch.

"Very well Haynes, I think you have decided your own fate. Private, when one of your mates relieves you, find a sack and tie it over his head. I will not have my men subjected to such treatment."

Phillips went back to the quarterdeck, and found the first lieutenant at the entry port, greeting some new arrivals. Wainright came over with a young man in a bottle green coat, and a sturdy middle aged seaman with a queue down his back, and a ribbon dangling from his cap with 'Triumphant' embroidered on it.

The seaman approached, took off his cap, knuckled his forehead, and stood before Phillips. "Sir Harder, captain of the maintop on Cossack, Cap'n Wilson, sir."

"I see, Harder. What brings you here?"

"Sir, Cap'n Wilson sir, he goes ashore and comes back and says the frigate goes into the dockyard. Crew goes into the receiving ship. He takes me aside and says this brig is fitting out foreign and needs some good seamen."

"That we do, Harder. Did you bring anyone with you?"

"Aye, that I did sir. Eight prime seamen, all able bodied."

"Well, I am glad to see you and your mates, Harder. If you will stand by, I will have my first officer get you settled in. In the meantime, I see that I have another guest."

"Aye sir, that is Doctor Fletcher, he was assistant surgeon aboard Cossack."

Phillips waited for the new surgeon, who approached and doffed his cap. Introducing himself. Phillips asked how he had come to be aboard the post ship Cossack.

Fletcher said he had been serving as a doctor on a large plantation on Barbados, caring for the slaves. Wishing to broaden his horizons he had asked for an appointment aboard a Royal Navy ship and had been granted an Assistant Surgeon's warrant and appointment to Cossack. Now that she was going into the dockyard for an indefinite period, he needed another ship.

Phillips examined the warrant. "This appears to have been issued by Governor Beckwith in Barbados last year. I am sure this was proper for your appointment aboard Cossack, but here in Portsmouth, I wonder if a warrant from the Sick and Hurt Board might be required."

'Sir, Captain Wilson on Cossack thought as long as I do not go ashore in Britain, my warrant from Governor Beckwith will remain valid."

Phillips thought about the matter. "As I do need a surgeon, I will take you aboard. I presume you do have your instruments and medications."

CHAPTER FOURTEEN

Phillips saw his first officer had finished with the new seamen from Cossack, and called him over. "Mister Wainright, you should know I am taking Doctor Fletcher on board as Assistant Surgeon on the strength of his warrant from Governor Beckwith of Barbados. I may be slapped on the wrist for this, but we do need a surgeon, and we must anticipate we will not continue swinging around the anchor much longer."

'Now we come to the matter of Landsman Haynes. I had hoped to avoid sending him ashore to await court martial, but that is not to be. When I saw him below earlier, he again displayed disrespect for me, and kicked our Master at Arms. I want you to meet with all that have been assaulted by the man and draw up charges. I will go over them and sign them when I am satisfied. I really hate to do this, but we cannot take this man on a long voyage at sea with him acting up like this."

Phillips was pulled ashore with a heavy heart. He knew he was carrying a man's life in the papers he carried, but had been not been able to find an alternative. Haynes was going to have to stand a court martial and take the consequences.

Entering the admiral's shore office, he was greeted by the same lamed lieutenant he had met before. He explained his mission, and the lieutenant asked to see the papers. Phillips handed him depositions from the various people aboard Alert who had come afoul of the man, from the Marine who had had his musket thrown overboard to his own statement.

The officer whistled. "This man is for the high jump. The admiral will never stand for this. Normally, he is reluctant to accept paperwork of this kind, but I think he must see this."

Phillips sat outside the room for an hour, waiting to be called. Finally, the clerk ushered him in.

Admiral Curtis was sitting at his desk, with the documents Phillips had brought before him. He looked up and said, "Captain Phillips, I have read over these papers, and wonder if you could tell me what is behind them. Why did this man do what he did?"

Phillips went over the events from the initial spitting on the deck, to the events in the mess deck. He assured the admiral that he had given the man every opportunity, but Haynes had refused every chance. He related how the man was now chained to the mess deck in shackles with a biscuit bag over his head because of his constant spitting at those passing by."

Admiral Curtis pondered. "We have just enough captains in harbor to convene an immediate court. We must get this done soon, as you will be sailing shortly."

"Sir, I wonder if I might bring up one more difficulty. An assistant surgeon came aboard yesterday from Cossack and asked to join. His warrant comes from the Governor of Barbados. He thinks as long as he does not go ashore, that warrant will remain valid."

Admiral Curtis said, "I think the man may be whistling in the wind. However, a Commissioner of the Transport Board has an appointment with me this afternoon. They have recently taken the Sick and Hurt people into their fold. We do not want to anger them. I will get his advice on the matter while we are waiting for the court martial proceedings to run their course."

Landsman Haynes was strapped to a carrying board and lowered into the waiting launch to be transferred to the old liner that was temporarily serving as the port admiral's flagship. Unrepentant, the man still tried to lash out at anyone passing close by. With his arms and legs lashed to the board, and a bag covering his head, he was unable to cause any more harm.

Alert's orders for the next mission were sent to the flag from the Admiralty. Like his previous trip to the Baltic, he found he would be carrying dispatches to Admiral Saumarez. Admiral Curtis called him to the flag's great cabin to give him the latest thoughts.

"Regarding your surgeon, Captain; an official will call on him later this afternoon to discover his qualifications and examine his surgical instruments and medicament supplies. Should these pass muster, his warrant will come before you sail. I told Commissioner Hendricks that surgeons willing to serve in the fleet were a rare breed, and we must try not let this man get away."

"Now then, regarding the court martial. We have several other matters hanging fire that need to be resolved in this court. Your prisoner however, will be the most important case, and will be tried first. We will start the proceedings early, so make sure all your people will be on hand."

"Now, I must warn you the surgeon of my flagship has examined the prisoner, and believes he has suffered an undue amount of injuries, almost as if he had been tortured. He was particularly upset about the gag in the fellow's mouth. Apparently his guards have tied an oak peg between his teeth, and the surgeon feels this must be very painful. He warns me that he may feel impelled to discuss this matter with the officer charged with the prisoner's defense."

"Sir, unless restrained, whenever the prisoner comes near another person, he tries to bite, kick or spit. The restraints we are using are intended to stop that nonsense."

"This matter will be discussed in the trial, Captain. We have no need of going over it here."

Captain Phillips returned to Alert and ordered all who would testify during the case to go over what he intended to say during the proceeding, and ensure what he had to say was indeed correct.

He called Doctor Fletcher to his cabin and informed him his equipment and medical supplies would be inspected the next day. Fletcher was indeed nervous over the prospect. He admitted purchasing the instruments over a period of time, where ever he could find something at a reasonable price. Many had been purchased in the Caribbean, used, and perhaps the quality was not of the best.

"Doctor", Phillips advised. "It is too late to correct matters now. You must stand or fall with what you have. However, assuming you do obtain your permanent warrant and go to sea with us, you may want to talk to our armorer. It is possible he can make a few useful tools for you."

The court proceedings began at the beginning of the forenoon watch, at 8:00, in the great cabin of the flagship. The five post captains serving as judges would sit at tables placed athwart ship before the stern windows. Benches had been placed in the rear for those having business before the court.

Phillips, his first officer and witnesses among the crew took up much of the seating space. The prisoner was marched in with two Royal Marine guards on either side. A young Navy lieutenant marched importantly in front with drawn sword.

The President of the court with the five post captains filed in and took their places at the tables. The commander who would prosecute the case stood by his seat in the front row, beside the Judge Advocate.

The Judge Advocate administered the oath to the officers of the court, and the proceedings began. Phillips had been informed he would be the first witness to testify, and he should remain in the cabin, while the others were removed until their testimony was needed.

While waiting for the excess people to remove themselves, Phillips was idly watching the prisoner. The shackles the new armorer had fabricated were intended to bolt permanently to the deck, Haynes had been released from them, and he had been brought to his court bound with line around his wrists and ankles, as well the bag over his head. Someone on the flag had replaced the line with iron shackles to his hands and feet.

Each circlet of iron around each ankle and wrist was connected to its mate with a length of light chain. His hands were shackled in front of his body, and he had a certain range of motion. Having informed the officers involved with the prisoner's security the details of his conduct aboard Alert, Phillips was surprised at Hayne's comparative freedom of movement.

At any rate, the man was no longer acting up, and the bag had been removed from his head.

Phillips was called forward to testify to the details of the man's conduct. After undergoing extensive questioning from several captains on the board, he thought he might be sent back to the wardroom, where the witnesses remained when not testifying. While the captains were discussing his testimony, one knocked over a pitcher of water on the table. The pitcher fell onto the deck and shattered. The court president impatiently called for somebody to clear away the debris.

The lieutenant supervising the prisoner's guards was the junior officer present, and thought it his duty to handle the situation. He ordered the two Marine guards to clear away the shards of broken glass and water, while he assumed custody of the prisoner. The Marines leaned their muskets against the table and went forward to see what was required

At that moment, the prisoner shoved the lieutenant aside using the force of his body, and slammed his chained fists against the officer's face. The lieutenant's sword fell from his hand, and with lightning fast reflexes, Haynes snatched it out of the air and took a swing at the officer. The lieutenant received a fearsome slash on the shoulder from the razor sharp blade, and fell to the deck.

Every officer present had a sword belted on and perhaps half had the presence of mind to draw his blade and attempt to stop the prisoner. Phillips had his own out and intended to run the fellow through to stop him for good.

Haynes, the sword in one hand, tried to secure one of the muskets with the other. When he clumsily knocked both to the floor, he started toward the judges with just the blade. A Marine captain there merely to observe, drew his own weapon and slashed Haynes leg as he passed. Hamstrung, the prisoner fell to the deck with a severed tendon and found himself with a dozen swords at his neck.

There was a recess while the ship's surgeon bound the fellow up, and servants set right the overturned benches. The defense submitted the trial should be delayed while the prisoner healed. The president of the court, with a cursory glance at the other judges, disposed of that plan. Captain Houze decreed, "The man has been treated and should not bleed to death during the trial. We will finish this and settle matters as soon as possible."

Since he had finished his testimony, Phillips was sent away with other witnesses and spectators and retired to the wardroom. An hour later, the wardroom servant entered and handed him a message from the flag captain. He was to report the flag captain on the liner's quarterdeck.

There, Captain Howze informed him the trial judges had decided to throw out all the charges pending except for the one filed by Captain Phillips regarding the prisoner's disrespect while another relating to the attack on Lieutenant Wilkerson had been added. Since the trial was still in the very early stages, the judge advocate had decided it was permissible to add the extra charge, rather than hold an entirely new court martial on that charge.

Having heard all the testimony they wished to hear, this proceeding was nearly over and the next case would begin shortly.

He did not know what to make of the dismissal of most charges. Surely the judges would not find Haynes 'Not Guilty'?

Captain Houze reassured him. "This fellow Haynes was certainly a bad bargain. It is the high jump for him! The admiral wished to apologize in advance for having the execution on the flagship rather than your brig."

"Sir, then the man has been found guilty?"

"Oh, not yet. We will let the sentencing go for a while. The admiral wants us to get some of the minor cases out of the way. We hope to have those completed by this afternoon, then Haynes will be brought back. We will hear a little more testimony considering the latest attack, then he will be found guilty and sentenced to hang. Admiral Curtis will sign the order immediately, and the prisoner will be taken on deck and the noose will be placed around his neck."

"It was thought we could use Wilkerson's injury as the excuse to delay the trial until the other cases had been decided. The fellow has apparently lost a lot of blood and can barely stand. That does not signify, however. He can be tied to a chair in court, and for that matter sit until he is hauled up to the main yard. The surgeon has him below now, but says he will be able to testify later this afternoon. Then we can pass sentence and take the prisoner on deck immediately to hang. The admiral feels this scenario will make a deeper impression on the men."

"We want you to return to Alert and send over a party of a dozen men, who will actually do the honors."

"If he wishes, Haynes may have a moment with the chaplain, then your party will tail onto the rope and walk off with it. His body will be left hanging from the main yardarm for the remainder of the day, so others may think twice before they violate the Twenty First Article of War."

"You understand, normally he would have been executed aboard your brig, since that is where most of the offenses occurred. In this case, Haynes actions were so infamous the admiral wished to impress others with the gravity of the offense by executing him on the flag immediately after sentencing."

"This additional charge was levied against the man after you left the court. This is the charge on which he will be found guilty. The others, except for the insolence charge you filed were dismissed so the court need not waste its time hearing testimony on a man it will hang anyway. You may go back to Alert now. You will muster your crew on deck when the time of execution draws near. Admiral Curtis wishes the men of every ship in harbor witness the execution. Your men will be returned after they have done their duty"

"Crews should be on deck facing the flag when the court martial flag is seen to dip. The execution will follow shortly.

Phillips was in his cabin going through the list of bosun's store that were needed. It seemed excessive, and knowing the habits of some bosun's, he wondered if some of these stores might be sold off the ship on a dark night to some shoreside speculator.

He decided he must soon give a clear warning to the crew of the penalties of such behavior. When Midshipman Akers breathlessly reported the court-martial flag had dipped, Phillips impulsively decided to make that announcement while both watches were drawn up on deck to witness the hanging. This might make a lasting impression on the men. He had no desire to see another man from the brig run up to a main yard.

Everyone in the harbor saw the smoke gush from the gun aboard the flag, and saw the bundle soar into the air aboard the flag, twisting and bending as it was hauled up. After several minutes, movement stopped, and Phillips addressed the crew. He reminded them of the consequences of thoughtless folly, and assured them that such could happen to men who committed common offenses, such as the theft of Crown property aboard ship.

He assured the crew that the mere theft of a few fathoms of line from ship's store could bring a man to court martial. With that, he dismissed the watch below, and summoned Mister Wainright into his cabin.

"Lieutenant, as soon as the mail bags and dispatch pouches come on board, I expect we will be ordered to sail for the Baltic."

CHAPTER FIFTEEN

Alert remained at anchor in Portsmouth Harbor, seemingly forgotten by the authorities. A few crewmen were sent aboard the brig, one of the more welcome additions being Master's Mate Wilcox, who would serve as the brig's sailing master. In addition, Doctor Fletcher's warrant had been approved, and he was now the brig's surgeon.

Finally, on a windy day that was threatening rain, a cutter made its way to the brig, hooked on about eight bells in the morning watch. A young midshipman clambered aboard in wrapped in a length of tarred sailcloth, and delivered a packet to the midshipman commanding the anchor watch.

This was immediately sent to Lieutenant Wainright, who saw it had come from the port admiral and immediately took it to his captain. Phillips had been up much of the night with the bosun who was concerned with the condition of the standing rigging of the foremast.

He had just dropped off to sleep when the package arrived. Cutting the twine with his pen knife, he opened the parcel and read the contents. He was directed to come ashore as soon as he had read the instructions and report to Admiral Curtis at the George Inn.

There was a flurry of activity as the boat crew donned the clothing they reserved for that duty, and the captain's servant brushed his coat. Phillips climbed down the side of the pitching brig, and made it into the boat without embarrassing himself. He took off his hat and put it under the boat cloak to prevent it from becoming soaked in the spray that was coming aboard.

His boat crew were all long service seamen that had volunteered to join, so he decided to trust them not to desert. Normally, a captain coming ashore, might order the boat to return to the ship, or at least remain offshore to inhibit desertion. He hated to see the men subjected to the foul weather any more than necessary.

They approached the lee side of the quay, where he handed the cox'n some money and told him to take the men to a nearby ordinary and stand them to a drink.

"No man is to become incapable though. We have to make it back to the brig when I am finished at the George. You had better take turns watching for me. We may have to leave in a rush. Someone will have to stay with the boat, also."

As the boat tied up and the crew began to disembark, the rain that had been threatening, finally came in a downpour. A single enclosed chaise stood under an overhang at the ordinary. As the men ran inside with a whoop, Phillips engaged the driver of the chaise to take him to the ordinary. The fellow was reluctant to leave his shelter, but agreed when Phillips offered to pay him half again what the fare was worth.

The horse drawing the chaise was reluctant also to go out into the rain, but a touch of the whip encouraged him.

Phillips felt like a drowned rat when he entered the inn. Despite his boat cloak, his hat and coat was drenched, and the inn's porter busied himself taking his outer garb and placing them before the fire. He took Phillips sword also, promising to dry the weapon so it would not rust.

The landlord came to him and led him to the room where Admiral Curtis was entertaining some local officials. The admiral appeared reluctant to go into any explanations while his civilian guests were present, so Phillips sat there drinking port, while everyone exchanged pleasantries.

It was an hour before the civilians called for their cloaks and departed. Phillips by now had found he was going to need to visit the 'jakes' soon, but decided he could forbear a little longer, when the admiral called for cigars and got down to business.

"Captain Phillips, my flag lieutenant will give you dispatches for Admiral Saumarez in the Baltic, which you will deliver. After that, you will place yourself under the admiral's orders, and join his fleet. You will find we are still at war with the Danes, and nobody knows which way the Swedes will go. Bonaparte is pressing them to declare war on us, but they enjoy our trade. Russia also is at war with us, but there are signs they may be moderating their views. The czar is not happy with the insults he has received from Bonaparte."

"Admiral Saumarez will be the arbiter there as how you should act. He is the local authority, and will decide which enemies we will prosecute vigorously, and which we will treat with some moderation. I think you will find the admiral, while he may be lenient toward a country we may nominally be at war with, will expect a similar leniency in return."

"Of course, we would not wish to drive a presently neutral country into enmity with us unnecessarily. Until Admiral Saumarez gives you appropriate guidance and orders, you will not unilaterally attack vessels flying the colors of Sweden or Russia. Should such vessels fire at you, you are, of course, free to respond accordingly."

"There is, of course, no doubt of Denmark's hostility. You may attack any Danish ships as you have occasion to do so."

"Earlier this year, we took the Danish island of Anholt, in the Kattegat in order to return the light there to operation. On your way to the Baltic, you will stop at Anholt and determine any needs of the garrison."

"Now, Mister Andrews should be outside with the dispatches. If you have no questions, you may return to your brig and sail as soon as wind and tide permit. You may just be able to beat out of the harbor with the wind we have now. I will not keep you any longer."

Alert made her way up the channel without coming into contact with any enemy vessels until she sailed past the Dutch coast. Two strangers came out to look at her. They both appeared to be privateers, and were flying the colors of the Batavian Republic, an ally of France. One was a brig, smaller than Alert. The other though, was a ship rigged corvette pierced for sixteen guns.

She would be a serious foe,by herself. Phillips thought it would be difficult to engage both privateers at once. Accordingly, he put the westerly wind on Alert's quarter, hoisted every scrap of canvas the brig could carry, and flew off to the north east.

The corvette had no trouble staying with her, but the little brig was having trouble, falling back farther every hour. The corvette for a while attempted to keep both her consort and the chase in sight, but when the brig's topsails dropped before the horizon, the corvette too, hoisted everything she could carry.

The corvette was just the slightest bit faster than Alert, and it soon became evident Alert could not outrace the slender corvette, so she came to, stripped down to fighting sails, and waited for her foe.

CHAPTER SIXTEEN

Phillips was doubting the wisdom of engaging this enemy. He was carrying dispatches, and knew Admiral Saumarez would have words with him if he thought Alert could have avoided the fight. With that in mind, he decided to open fire with his few long guns when the corvette came in range. He thought the captain of that corvette might have assumed the brig was an unarmed trading vessel. Perhaps finding her quarry had teeth would cause her to sheer off and seek easier prey.

The two long six pounders at bow and stern erupted, without the enemy taking notice. The gun crews had not been properly worked up, so their accuracy was poor. They continued banging away with no apparent distress to the enemy. Mister Wainright had been taking sightings of her masthead with his sextant, and when he reported she was within range, he ordered the new carronades prepared.

Most regarded the light, short barreled weapons to be inaccurate, only useful in close range fighting. Phillips had studied the guns though, and found, while the range was shorter than long guns throwing the same weight ball, the ball did fit more closely in the bore of the gun, eliminating some inaccuracy there, and utilizing the small powder charge more efficiently. In addition, the carronades had at least rudimentary sights, with an elevation screw, rather than relying on a wooden quoin to adjust elevation, as was necessary with the long guns.

Thus far on the short voyage, he had not had a chance to give the new crew much chance to work with the new guns, merely running them in and out a few times every day. There had been no opportunity to lay in a store of privately owned ammunition for the crew to use for live fire practice.

He did, however, have a gunner's mate, who claimed to have served with his own father, Captain John Phillips, and was supposedly well versed on the carronade. Orson was ordered to go from gun to gun on the broadside, firing each carronade individually, taking especial care with the aim.

Orson stood at the forward carronade, starboard side and waited for the order. Phillips nodded at Mister Wainright, and at his signal, Orson looked down the sight, waiting for the brig to rise on a swell. As it did, he yanked on the firing lanyard, and the gun fired, recoiling back on its slide.

Phillips was watching through his glass, and saw the brief plume of spray when the ball hit the sea close aboard the corvette. Orson had immediately gone to the next gun and fired that. The ball from this shot struck the sea just short of the corvettes bow.

Shot after shot went toward the enemy, as she approached. Finally, one ball did not produce a splash. It had evidently struck the target ship. Phillips could make out a flurry of activity on her forward deck, as though the high angled shot had hit her deck. More shots began hitting the corvette, which became tired of this treatment, and came about to fire her own broadside. Only one round of the eight fired struck, and that had ricocheted from the surface of the sea, and struck the brig's beam under the quarterdeck.

Phillips was close to the impact site and saw the eight pound ball adhering in the timber for a moment before it fell back into the sea.

The brig's guns on the starboard side were all firing now, under the control of their own gun captains, and the heavy balls were doing serious damage to the corvette. The enemy gunners were having difficulty hitting the brig, and their small eight pound balls did much less damage when they did strike.

As the thirty two pound balls kept impacting the enemy at a furious rate, he noticed some of the loaders were tiring from handling the heavy ammunition. He sent Mister Akers around to each gun, telling the crews to change positions. Men standing by the unused port guns were brought over to spell the starboard gunners.

In the midst of this activity, a glance at the enemy showed men scrambling into the tops to take in sail. While occupied with this, the enemy's mainmast was seen to begin to lean, then it fell with a rush over the side. The enemy tried to get herself under control, leaving the men in the water behind clinging to the wreckage with the ship turning to port in an effort to escape.

Phillips now had the opportunity to leave the enemy behind and continue on his voyage, which he knew would meet with the approval of the Admiralty. However, he considered the corvette was within easy reach of several ports on the continent and should she make one of them safely, could be repaired and be back preying upon British commerce within a few weeks.

With that in mind, he ordered Alert put on a course to intercept the corvette and came up on her bow. The enemy vessel was still trying to get herself in some kind of order. Her starboard fore chains had been struck, and her shrouds were loose there. With the foremast starting to lean, she was in serious trouble.

Ordering all guns to load with grape, Phillips eased the brig closer, and fired a single blast of grape at the crewmen working on the rigging. A swirl in the crowd left a half dozen men on the deck. There was quiet for a moment. The enemy had no guns that would bear and Alert was waiting. Finally, the tricolor came fluttering down and the fight was over.

Phillips told his first officer, "Mister Wainright, I would like you to take a party over and take command of the corvette. Have all small arms laid on the deck or thrown over the side with the men sent below. I'll send over some swivels that you can direct at the hatches in case any of them changes their mind. Better take Able Seaman Harder with you. He's probably one of the best people we have on Alert. Try not to lose him to another captain. When you are prepared to sail, we will part company and you may take her back home."

Alert's captain waited a glass for word to come back. Finally, Mister Akers came back in the jolly boat and reported.

"Sir, there has been fearsome damage done to the corvette. Mister Wainright has the French carpenter's crew working at patching the worst shot holes, but wishes you to send over our own carpenter. He does not trust the Frenchmen to do a proper job.'

Leaving Mister Wilcox in charge of the brig, Phillips went over to the corvette with the carpenter and his crew, as well as the bosun. The ship had received some serious damage, but the French carpenter's crew, warned they would go to the bottom with the ship should they not get her wounds repaired, had already made great strides in getting her seaworthy.

Alert's crew stepped in and began working on the fore chains, while the bosun supervised the repair of the standing rigging. By late afternoon, the foremast had lost its list to port, and become erect again. After Wainright and Phillips discussed the matter, it was decided the corvette would be able to make a British port without her mainmast.

Wainright was eager to take her in, since it was not unknown for a first officer to be promoted to commander after such a battle. Before she left, Captain Phillips had some of her powder removed and placed in Alert's magazine. Her eight pound balls would fit none of Alert's guns, but he did have all her grape loads brought over. The bosun and gunner's mates would break down these loads and use the shot to make charges to fit Alert's guns.

CHAPTER SEVENTEEN

After parting, Alert continued northward toward the entrance to the Kattegat, while the corvette sailed south east toward Britain. Having already made the trip once in Alert, Phillips thought he knew what to expect. Rounding the Skaw into the Kattegat, he kept as close to the Swedish coast as he could. He knew the Danish batteries would fire on his ship, but was fairly sure the Swedes would not. Once through the entrance, it was clear sailing, as clear of course, as any could be in the treacherous waters of the Kattegat.

When Anholt Island appeared, Alert backed her topsails to wait for a boat seen putting off from shore. The Royal Marine lieutenant in the boat delivered a letter and asked it be taken to Admiral Saumarez. The officer reported the anticipated supply ship had never arrived and the garrison was very low on supplies. The people were largely subsisting on locally caught fish and hoped for something better to supplement their diet.

Phillips promised to bring the matter to the admiral's attention, and in the meantime offloaded a few casks of salt beef and some biscuit for their immediate needs. After wishing the Marine and his men well, and assuring him he would stop by on his return voyage, he advised his sailing master of the difficulties of the entrance into the Baltic. The narrow strait between Swedish Helsingborg and Danish Helsingor was only a few miles wide, and dominated by guns on both shores.

The Marine they had just spoken to assured them Sweden was not yet at war with Britain, but Denmark certainly was. After discussing the matter, it was decided Alert would hoist Swedish colors and attempt to pass the strait into the Baltic in the very early morning hours.

Alert's captain was unsure how this strategy would develop. The Swedes might very well take offence at their effrontery, but he thought he would just hoist his red ensign if approached by a Swedish gunboat and ignore them. Hopefully, by the time anyone could take any great offence, they would be out into the reaches of the Baltic, and out of mind of the Swedish authorities ashore.

In any event, they sailed through the narrow strait after dark and while a few shots were fired from the Danish side, they heard or saw nothing from Sweden.

It was a few weeks before they discovered the location of Admiral Sauvarez and his fleet. Alert hailed a British flagged Baltic trader that was waiting for the convoy to form for the homeward voyage. The trader informed them the fleet had been sighted off Tallinn near the Gulf of Finland. Proceeding on their way, they encountered the

Camilla frigate who confirmed the location of the flag, and gave its probable location.

Alert made her number to HMS Victory soon after, and her captain was directed to repair on board. Admiral Saumarez was anxious for news from home, and eagerly accepted his own personal mail as well as the official dispatches. He excused himself while he read over the more important and bade his servant to fill Phillip's glass and supply him with a light lunch.

When finished, Admiral Saumarez apologized for his discourtesy, mentioning it had been a long period without word from his family. He got to the point: "Captain Phillips, I see that I am to take Alert under my orders. She will undoubtedly be valuable for delivering my communications."

"For now though, I see from the report you just delivered, the garrison on Anholt is short of provisions. It is important for the fleet for that garrison to remain in being. Navigational difficulties in the Kattegat being what they are, it is important the light on the island be kept burning for the safety of our country's trade, as well as the fleet."

"Therefore, I will use your brig to bring immediate relief to the island. I have a contract with a supplier in Karlskrona in Sweden to furnish us with ship's biscuit. A supply has recently reached us, and we will supply you with a few tons of biscuit, and some cabbages for Anholt."

"Additionally, I am furnishing you a purse of coin to purchase cattle on the Danish Island of

Bornholm. A man by the name of Kofoed, in the village of Pedersker, on the southern coast of Bornholm Island, has dealt with us honestly before. While the island is of course Danish, the area is sparsely inhabited, and I believe if you refrain from showing the national colors needlessly, you will not attract undue attention."

"In your orders, you will find reference to the signal you will fly upon reaching the designated point on the coast. It may be necessary to return several times, in case Mister Kofoed or one of his people does not notice your brig or signal in your first visit. Remember, these are farming people as well as fishermen, with little knowledge of naval affairs. You may purchase whatever cattle you can take aboard your brig, as well as any vegetables they may have for sale."

"After taking your cargo on board, you may make for Anholt Island with all due haste, and re-supply the garrison there. After completing this mission, you will return to me. Providing you have no important dispatches aboard, you may cause any disruption possible against enemy commerce. Should any British naval officer more senior than yourself venture to order you to any duty not ordered by myself, you may do so, providing you take measures to inform my flag of the duty required. If you will wait on the quarterdeck, flags will see these orders put in writing, and having read and understood them, you may depart."

Before leaving Victory, Phillips had taken the opportunity to discuss the matter of approaching Bornholm with the flag's sailing master. This worthy assured him much of the Danish naval forces at present consisted of gunboats. "As long as you are not becalmed or trapped in shallow waters, you should be in no danger. They generally mount a heavy gun in their stern, but understand they can come about in a flash. If you determine they are Danes, take no nonsense from them. Approach them bows on if you get a chance, and give them a broadside when you pass."

Alert left the fleet bound for Bornholm. Since their destination was on the southern coast, she approached from that direction. From a pair of fishing boats netting herring off that coast, it was learned that Mister Kofoed was indeed located there and he could be notified of their presence for a fee. A few silver shillings to each boat captain got their assurance Kofoed would be notified to watch for their signal two days from hence, and no Danish or French military or naval authorities would be notified.

Alert went back out to sea and patrolled the remainder of the day and the next. No ship was spotted Phillips wished to interfere with, and he approached the south coast of Bornholm early on the second morning.

The agreed upon signal was the Blue Peter with an interrogative, which would be meaningless to anyone other than the recipient. With his sailing master watching the leadsman, and comparing the depths to those shown on his chart, Alert crept closer to the shore. Taking bearings from two buildings on shore that had been specified in his written orders, Alerts topsails were backed, and she slowed to a halt, waiting to see what developed on-shore.

An hour after displaying the signal, a small, gaff-rigged sloop left its harbor and put out to sea. When it appeared to be heading for them, Phillips went to his cabin to don his best coat and hat and buckle on his sword.

Wilcox, the sailing master and now acting lieutenant hailed the vessel as it drew near. A sturdy man of middle years, on the deck of the sloop announced in good English that he was Mister Kofoed.

Kofoed boarded Alert, and Phillips took him into the cabin. Over cigars given him by Admiral Saumarez, Phillips discussed the purchase of cattle and vegetables. Kofoed assured him he could furnish any number of young bullocks, as well as perhaps a ton of potatoes. A price was settled, and it was determined each load would be paid for as it was loaded aboard Alert.

That afternoon, two lighters came alongside with their loads of bawling cattle. Each animal had to have a canvas strap secured under its belly, and hoisted aboard with tackle from the mainyard. The carpenter and his mates were busy fabricating pens to hold the livestock.

With as many bullocks aboard as could be crowded on deck, one of the lighters made a trip with a load of potatoes. This lighter also carried Mister Kofoed and a well-built young man and a flaxen haired young woman, not yet twenty, judged Phillips.

Phillips was anxious to get away from the land, in case any Danish patrols came by, but invited Kofoed and his company on board. Inviting them into his cabin, his servant poured aquavit for the men and sherry for the woman.

Kofoed explained a problem he had. The two young people were his niece and nephew, his dead brother's children. The man was due to be conscripted into the army, which meant he might soon be fighting in one of Bonaparte's legions. The woman was being pursued by a French officer who was becoming too persistent.

It was felt the two should leave Bornholm, but where to go? Another relative, years before, had emigrated to America, and it was thought advisable this brother and sister should go there also. Kofoed said he would return the money paid for the provisions, if Alert would carry the pair to Britain, where they could take ship to the new world.

Phillips waved off the offer of payment, offering instead the advice the siblings might find the money useful on their journey.

Privately, Phillips was dubious. He wondered how the Royal Navy would accept the news that a young lady had been occupying his quarters, but decided to agree to their request. Kofoed was undoubtedly on good terms with Admiral Saumarez, and it would probably be wise to go along. Perhaps he could transfer his guests to Victory when he completed his mission to Anholt and returned to the fleet.

For now, he had the carpenter install a partition through the middle of his cabin, and Hilda, the young woman, was put in one, while her brother Hans slept in the other. Phillips moved into the tiny dog kennel of a cabin Lieutenant Wainright had occupied before he took the prize corvette back home.

The heavily laden brig worked her way to sea and set course for the Oresund, the narrow strait between Sweden and Zealand. Alert had already traversed this several times before, now she must do it again. This time, knowing Sweden was neutral, he put into Helsingborg and engaged a pilot to see them safely through the Oresund. They made it hugging the Swedish shore and entered the Kattegat without alerting the Danish batteries on Zealand.

The heavily laden brig was in no condition to seek a confrontation with anyone, and Mister Wilcox, their sailing master ordered the lookouts to be especially vigilant. Any sail sighted brought a change of course to put it under the horizon. It was a relief for the entire crew when Anholt Island came in sight.

CHAPTER EIGHTEEN

A channel through the shallows had been marked with buoys, and the brig made her way close to shore. A frigate was anchored farther out, and Hans approached Phillips, wondering if that ship might be returning to Britain. It had been intended that he and his sister would return to the Baltic with Alert, and travel to Britain at some time in the future. Perhaps they could shortcut the process and journey there earlier.

Phillips went to shore with his passengers, being met by the Royal Marine officer commanding the garrison, and Captain Davis from HMS Dido, 28 guns, 9 pounders. Davis had a request that was more of an order. He was on his way to the fleet in the Baltic, but the Anholt garrison commander had asked him to deliver a Danish official to London.

It seemed this person was an important personage in the French controlled Danish government, but had decided he no longer wished to serve Bonaparte. The official had sailed his own boat to Anholt, knowing the island was in British hands. He had in his possession quantities of French and Danish government documents HM Government would doubtless like to have.

Since he could not in good conscience turn about himself and retrace his steps, the frigate captain was asking Alert to do just that. He felt Admiral Saumarez rather have Dido available than Alert. After thinking about the matter, Phillip decided his orders from the admiral allowed for just such an eventuality. He agreed to the mission, but requested Captain Davis inform Admiral Saumarez of the situation.

While he had the chance, he wrote the admiral explaining his reasons and informed him he had Kofoeds's niece and nephew on board who also wished to go to Britain.

The frigate off loaded her passenger and set sail for the Baltic next morning, while Alert began unloading her cargo. Only moments after the first beasts were landed, the crew of Alert heard the commotion as the first bullock was dispatched and butchered for the troop's noon meal.

The men of Alert were given a few days for a run on-shore, there being little chance for anyone to desert. The Royal Marine garrison kept the men away from the few Danish inhabitants, their commanders not wanting to have any incidents.

With another passenger to find space for, Phillips moved out of the first lieutenant's nook, and slung a hammock in the little cranny his clerk and servant had occupied previously. With a hard heart, he sent them to the mess deck with the seamen.

Olaf Lund, the refugee official, seemed astonished to see the tiny space he was to occupy on the voyage back to Britain , but luckily he spoke very good English, and Phillips was able to assure him he had lived in that same space for over a week.

On fair weather days, the passengers spent much of their time on the quarterdeck where they learned a bit about each other and the officers. Phillips learned Hilda was his own age, and missed her uncle and aunt. He had already observed the woman was very attractive indeed, but learning of her unpleasant experiences with the French officer back in Bornholm, he tried to hide his interest.

She was interested in the ship, so he spent time with her, explaining the sails and rigging, and showing her how to use the sextant.

Her brother Hans, became almost an un-official midshipman. He was already well versed on seamanship, having sailed of fishing boats since he was young. Not being on the books, of course he could not engage in any official duties, but he often served as assistant to the deck officer on watches.

With the extra ammunition gained from the captured corvette earlier in the voyage, he was able now to exercise his people using live fire. Young Hans Kofoed took part in the practice. By the time they reached Portsmouth Harbor, the men were becoming proficient with the guns.

Alert made her number entering harbor and saluted the flag. When her captain was ordered to report to the flag, Phillips took his passengers along. Admiral Curtis had little to say to the siblings, but Mister Lund interested him greatly. He immediately put Phillips on leave and ordered him to escort Lund to London.

"You may as well take the Kofoeds there, also. Perhaps someone in Admiralty might want to talk to them."

It was a grueling, all-day ride to London. Phillips and Hans initially rode on top, leaving the interior for Lund, Hilda and another passenger. At the first stop though, Hilda insisted she ride on top, also. Hans and Phillips learned the other passenger had been annoying Hilda. Hans and Timothy discussed the matter and decided it was not the time to be challenging anyone.

The two did discuss the matter with the portly civilian offender, and assured him it would be better all-around if he did not speak with the woman for the remainder of the trip.

Both were well built young men and Phillips of course had his blade belted on, so the individual quickly apologized and assured them he would not speak to Hilda again. The driver became involved in the discussion and it was decided it would be better if Hilda remained inside. Her brother would join her, and the offending stranger was exiled to the top with Phillips.

The coach arrived in London at nightfall, too late to visit the Admiralty. The siblings were concerned with spending their limited supply of money, so Phillips offered them rooms in his family's townhouse, which was usually vacant with his father at sea so much. Lund had a lodging warrant from the port admiral and elected to stay at the coaching inn, agreeing to meet with the others at the Admiralty on the morrow.

A two horse enclosed 'growler' coach for hire came by and the trio engaged it to take them to the house. Phillips had to hammer on the door for a lengthy period before the maid opened it. The butler stood behind her with a short barreled musketoon, primed and ready.

Ther was a tense moment or two before the butler recognized young Master Timothy, all grown and in the King's uniform. It was then necessary for all the help in the house to be called an re-introduced to the young master.

Tim explained the situation, and was assured rooms would be prepared in a few minutes. In the meantime, they were shown into the parlor, and the housekeeper came in with keys to the wine cabinet and produced the tea caddy.

Hilda was exhausted from the coach travel and asked the maid to show her to her room as soon as it was ready. Phillips found his father's cigars and trimmed the ends from two. Neither young man was a confirmed cigar smoker, but they lit their tobacco from a shared spill and coughed away. They each had a brandy before the two retired for the night. The brandy put Timothy to sleep at once.

CHAPTER NINETEEN

Next morning, Tim and Hans rose early before the rest of the household, and breakfasted from the offerings of a street side pieman. From another peddler, they each had a pint of beer, and then they were ready to meet their masters in the Admiralty.

Since Hans was not knowledgeable in the ways of that organization, Tim took the lead. Explaining their business to a porter, they were directed to the waiting room. Even this early, the seats were nearly all taken. Seeing a pair of post captains entering, Phillips steered Hans away from the only two seats left occupied and they stood against the wall.

There they remained all morning, occasionally spelling each other when it became time to visit the necessary or to refresh their thirst. By afternoon, Hans had become impatient and irritable, deciding he was not going to wait for the Navy any longer. He decided he was going to the docks and see about obtaining passage to America for himself and his sister.

Nothing Phillips could say would dissuade him and he was determined to leave. When he found a ship, he would find his way back to the house and collect his sister.

The pair had noticed a thin man, balding and rather fragile looking appearing in the waiting room now and again all morning, speaking to every post captain in the room. As they neared the door, the fellow approached Tim.

"Lieutenant, I am attempting to find a Captain Phillips. Would you know of him and where he might be found?"

"Captain Phillips", wondered Tim. "Would that be Captain John Phillips or might it be Captain Timothy Phillips?"

"Oh sir; Captain Timothy Phillips, to be sure."

"Well sir, I am Timothy Phillips. Although I am a mere lieutenant, I command His Majesty's Brig Alert, and people do call me Captain sometimes."

"Sir, I humbly beg your pardon. His Lordship the Honorable Viscount Eckersley has been waiting for you all morning. He is most displeased."

"I too have been waiting all morning with Mister Kofoed here also, and we are both most displeased."

The two were ushered into a paneled office with an enormous desk. Phillips reported to the official and both men were requested to sit. Eckersley referred to the long wait both parties had experienced and said, "That fool Watson was told to bring in Captain Phillips and party. He approached every post captain that entered the building. It escaped him that officers without post captain epaulettes could also be addressed as Captain."

He mentioned he had spent an hour earlier with Mister Lund and examined the documents he had brought from Denmark. Eckersley said both Lund and those documents were going to be very useful. Lund had been offered a paid position as an advisor on the Baltic region for the Admiralty, which had been accepted.

After discussing Danish affairs with Hans, Eckersley informed him that he was probably not going to be needed on an advisory position, but perhaps there might be another position open to a well-built young man.

"I am required to be escorted by an armed guard whenever I carry secret documents. My present man was injured when a footpad attempted to take my case a few evenings ago. Jenkins is mobile, and still accompanies me but his arm was broken. Would you consider assisting him to escort me?"

It was soon settled. Hans would enter the employ of Viscount Eckersley. His sister also, might be considered as a companion for his wife. They were requested to bring her to the house that very night.

"Now then, Captain Phillips, what are we to do with you?"

Phillips sat mute. As a naval officer he had not expected he would have any input as to his assignments.

Eckersley went on, "I believe you were sent here by the Portsmouth Port Admiral in case you were needed to elaborate on anything Lund or young Kofoed might have to say. The documents Lund brought were self-explanatory, and his own accounts were perfectly clear. I doubt we will need further clarification. I believe you are assigned to Admiral Saumarez in the Baltic, is that not so?"

'Yes sir, my brig Alert, is mostly utilized for delivering dispatches and transporting supplies."

"Ah yes, I am told you young firebrands are always champing at the bit to engage enemy vessels and gain glory for yourselves. I would imagine duties such as you describe must inhibit chances for action."

"Young man, while the duties the Navy has assigned you to perform are most important, so is the hindrance of Bonaparte's commerce. Every French trading vessel or one belonging to any ally that is captured or destroyed is a spoke in the French economic wheel."

"Admiral Saumarez has indicated he needs more seamen for his fleet to replace men lost from injury or disease. Every ship we send to him, we endeavor to put extra men aboard."

"Captain, where exactly is your brig anchored?"

"Portsmouth Harbor, Milord."

"Ah, I was hoping you were in the Pool or perhaps at the Nore. Well, we will give you your orders here, and you may draw on the Impress Service in Portsmouth for fifty additional hands.

Your brig is being sent back to the Baltic, but on the way there, your orders will give you a free hand in pursuing enemy ships and trade."

"You will have extraordinary freedom to bring discomfort to the enemy. Of course, the extra hands are intended to go to Admiral Saumarez, but you will be permitted to utilize some to send valuable prizes back home. Notice I said valuable. You will not regard this as a license to send back every fishing boat or small barge you capture. These you may sink or burn."

"Now, Captain Phillips, are there any questions? If not, stop by the Admiralty tomorrow morning and collect your orders and travel voucher."

That evening, Hans and Hilda visited Viscount Eckersley's home and Hilda was interviewed. With satisfaction on both sides, it was decided the siblings would present themselves there the next morning for duty. Phillips would bid them goodbye tonight, since he must return to the Admiralty early the next morning.

The orders when Phillips collected them surprised him. All was as the Viscount had related to him the previous day, but Alert was not to sail for another two weeks. He was to await the arrival of the mail packet from Lisbon. Apparently news being carried aboard was to be sent on to Saumarez.

He decided to spend a few days in London then coach back to Portsmouth in case anything needed his attention. He was particularly concerned over the whereabouts of Mister Wainright, his first officer. He had no word of him since he took command of the prize corvette earlier.

CHAPTER TWENTY

Orders and documents in hand, he returned to the house. It was now early in the afternoon, and the Portsmouth coach had already left. He settled in his library with a glass of wine and decided to read over his orders and instructions. Midway through, he was interrupted by the maid who presented him with a letter. It bore a private seal he did not recognize. The maid clarified, "It was a military gentleman that brought it. Royal Marine he said he was!"

Tim opened it and found he was being informed of a gathering the Viscountess was holding in two days' time. He was invited to attend.

What to wear for the event? Any of his old civilian clothing he had in the house was out of style and in any event, too small. He would have to appear in uniform. Luckily, it was in good enough condition and the maid assured him the women would get it in good order for the party.

When the time came, a cabriolet had been laid on, and he boarded the little two wheeled conveyance looking his best. The Viscount's doorman greeted him at the door and took his hat and sword. A maid led him back to the garden where the glittering guests were gathered around small tables covered with various foods. Apparently, one was supposed to take a plate and a servant at each table would supply you with your wants.

Another servant wended his way among the throng carrying a large tray of filled wine glasses. Not knowing the drill, Tim helped himself to a glass of wine, and waited to see what might develop.

Standing near one of the tables, he felt a feminine hand touch his arm. He turned and saw Susanne Wilder! She wore a fetching and revealing white gown and was easily the most alluring woman he saw present. Behind her was a gathering of older officers, of post rank and above and not a few apparent wives were glaring their displeasure.

Knowing better than to interfere with superior officer's intents, Phillips politely greeted her by name and tried to withdraw. She was having none of this though, and maneuvered him toward a group of seats near the edge of the garden. Two women seated there sniffed when Susanne bade him sit and hurriedly jumped up to relate this to their peers.

Susanne had him pinned there in the little seat, standing in front of him with her breast nearly in his face.

Desperately, he looked around and spotted Hans Kofoed entering the garden looking handsome in some kind of livery. He interrupted Miss Wilder in the middle of her account of a local scandal, and excused himself, almost knocking her over as he jumped up.

Rushing over to Hans, he shook his friend's hand and indicated the pouting woman behind him. "Hans, you should go meet that woman. I think you might get lucky!"

"I can't do that, old fellow. I am one of the servants here, and must not become familiar with the guests. My sister is coming behind me, why don't you talk with her. They don't regard her as a servant, being the Viscountess' companion.

Phillips saw Hilda being escorted down the path by a pair of fops much too old for her. Tim rushed to her side and offered to get her a glass of wine. The panicked look she had on her face disappeared and she said, "Tim, I don't need any wine but I would like it if you would sit with me."

The fops glared at him as they went looking for other prey, and Phillips led Hilda to the same group of seats he had just left. Susanne had left to find another victim and the two spent much of the evening discussing matters of interest to them.

Even after the rest of the party moved indoors when it grew chilly, they remained. Phillips noticed her shivering and took off his heavy coat and draped it over her shoulders. Before the evening was over, they discovered they both wanted to continue their friendship, and Tim told her she could write to him aboard HMS Alert in care of the Admiralty.

"It may take months before one of your letters reaches me, and more months before I can reply, but I will do so, Hilda."

Becoming more used to each other, they began recounting amusing things that had happened to themselves recently. She told him about the fops. They were as old as her uncle but had somehow thought if they persisted long enough one of them might be successful.

Her brother had approached them, but they dismissed him as one of the servants and threatened to have some bully boys thrash him. As new arrivals in London, neither knew what to do.

Phillips offered to call them out. Distraught, she begged him not to do that. "I hear both have been out many times, and are deadly with both pistol and sword. Please promise you will not do any such thing!"

As an alternative, Tim suggested she speak with the Viscountess. Perhaps she might have some advice on the matter. In the meantime, she should not go out un-escorted.

It was getting late and the stars had come out when Susanne made another attempt. She came out of the house, marched straight up to Tim and said, "Dear, I must really go home now. Would you please escort me?" She reached around Hilda and clutched his arm as she spoke.

Seeing the pair of fops coming out of the house with no prey to take home, Tim was inspired. "Susanne, I know those two gentlemen would be glad to escort you. Would you like me to call them over?"

Infuriated, Susanne ran back into the house. Finding Hans standing like a statue observing, Phillips went to him and told him he too must leave. He wanted to get on the early Portsmouth coach the next morning. Could he escort his sister to her room?

After leaving, while waiting for a cabriolet to happen by, Phillips kept his eyes open and his hand on his sword. He had made some enemies this night.

CHAPTER TWENTY ONE

It was early evening the next day when the coach arrived at the Portsmouth dockyard. He begged a ride in another ship's launch out to Alert. When he answered to the anchor watch's hail, he saw in the fading daylight a strange officer on the quarterdeck. The lieutenant was at the entryway to greet him when he came aboard. "Lieutenant Prescott, sir", he said, introducing himself. "Your new first officer."

"I am very happy to see you, Mister Prescott. Have you any news of my previous first?"

"I do, sir. I was told he was given command of a gun brig himself, as a reward for his part in the action you had with a French corvette."

"I am sorry that he will not be coming back to us. However, I am sure you will be an exemplary replacement. Have you had any information about our forthcoming mission?"

"No, sir."

"It will be the Baltic. Alert has been there several times before. We will deliver mail and dispatches, as well as some extra hands the Impress Service will hand over to us. These are intended for the fleet but we will have use of some of them should we take any prizes on the way."

"We will be sailing under Admiralty orders and have their lordship's permission to discomfit Napoleon's commerce as best we can. We will be permitted to send valuable prizes home, utilizing some of our extra hands, if necessary."

"Now Mister Prescott, have you had any warning as to when these hands will be coming aboard?"

"No sir, your news is the first I have heard of the extra men. Yesterday, beef and pork in casks came aboard, and our master's mate has it stowed below. I am told the water hoy will be alongside at first light tomorrow to top off our water."

"It looks like you have matters well in hand, Mister Prescott. We will not be leaving until the Lisbon mail packet comes in. It seems we will be carrying some dispatches from the Peninsula to the Baltic. Hopefully, the extra men will not appear until just before we leave. I need not tell you that the men will be jammed in like peas in a bag."

"Sir, I neglected to tell you four midshipmen came aboard the day before yesterday."

"What may I expect from them, Mister Prescott? Are they children right from their mother's arms or are they old enough that we may get some use from them?"

"Sir. Two of them seem to be seamen. The other pair have a year or two at sea.'

"Very well. We may be needing some of these young gentlemen for prizemasters. You will want to give each as much responsibility as he can handle. If one appears to be an ignorant dolt, tell me before we leave so I can set him ashore. We will have no space for useless hands on this voyage."

The days passed rapidly. The crew drilled incessantly at the various shipboard tasks, including daily gun drill. Of course, in harbor, it was impossible to actually fire the guns, but they were now being readied for simulated firing in record time.

Phillips had gone ashore to make some purchases for the next voyage, and discussed with the outfitter his need to obtain balls to fit his thirty two pounder carronades. Because Admiralty was parsimonious about supplying ammunition for practice purposes, if a captain wished to do very much live-fire practice, it was necessary to purchase his own ammunition.

The outfitter thought a moment and said it was possible a man he knew might be able to help. That evening, a sailing barge appeared off the larboard beam, and the anchor watch was asked to inform the captain.

Midshipman Kearns, one of the new mids come aboard and old enough in the service to take no nonsense, offered to drop a ball through the bottom of the boat if it did not leave.

A passenger in the boat assured the mid the captain indeed would wish to talk with him, so Kearns sent Mister Midshipman Halliday, one of the youngsters, to inform the captain. "Better for this lad to get his ears burned than himself", thought Kearns.

Captain Phillips surprised him by welcoming the man in the boat aboard and taking him to his cabin. Shortly after, the man was tucking a wad of currency into his coat pockets, while Midshipman Kearns was ordered to call the watch below. In the bottom of the barge was a quantity of thirty two pound balls. A line from tackle on the mainyard hauled aboard a cargo net filled with the heavy balls, and seamen carried each ball below one at a time.

It was necessary to repeat the operation several times before the barge was empty. Mister Prescott had appeared on deck as soon as the first balls came aboard and supervised the operation. As soon as the barge had left, and the deck had been swabbed down, dried and the men sent below, Phillips invited Prescott into his cabin for a drink.

"Mister Prescott, when you get a chance, take a look at a few of those balls. To me they looked to be in perfect condition. I would not be surprised if they came direct from the Carron Company in Falkirk."

Lieutenant Prescott's face remained blank so Phillips explained further. "You know of course of our difficulty with obtaining practice ammunition from the Admiralty. It is my custom to try to purchase such from private sources whenever I can. At this time, I need no powder since I obtained a quantity from the corvette we took on our last voyage."

"Normally, the only balls I can find are defective or badly rusted. These are new, and without a blemish. I suspect there may be a captain in the anchorage who has signed for a consignment of balls without counting them. Probably his gunner has made some extra income."

"Sir, should we not report this to the admiral?"

"There is that, Mister Prescott. However, we would then see the ammunition seized and my money would be gone. We would see a gunner lose his warrant and a captain made a mockery. Perhaps an enemy may escape our intentions because of our poor accuracy with the guns. I assure you, Mister Prescott, these balls will be fired at the enemy, rather than rusting in storage below. Perhaps the King's money will prove to be well spent."

The day came when the awaited dispatches were brought to the ship. On the same day, fifty hands were ushered aboard by the Impress Service. Few were impressed. Many of them were criminals of one sort or another who had spent weeks or months in gaol. A few were actual seamen who had been taken when their merchant ship arrived in port. Some of them seized by the Press before they had received their pay or had a run on shore.

It was time for Alert to sail.

The brig sailed over to run along the French coast. Pickings would be slim there since the Channel Fleet would have taken whatever shipping they could find. However, Phillips had learned the fleet was looking for some French ships of the line that had escaped from the Mediterranean earlier, and few British liners remained on blockade. Some of the smaller ports were not guarded and Phillips wondered if some shipping might take the opportunity to get to sea.

Off Dunkirk they had their first sighting of a profitable target. The masthead reported four sails to starboard, close in to the land. Master's Mate Wilcox had his chart laid on the binnacle when Phillips approached. By now the lookout had reported the vessels were coming toward them.

Wilcox opined, "Sir, they won't know who we are. They might think we are only a small trading brig, and thing it un-necessary to evade us. When we close though, if they become concerned, they could duck into this little bay just ahead. The chart shows it is defended by a small battery."

"If we can get a bit closer before they smoke us, we will be able to cut them off from the port.

As the strangers approached, two ship-rigged vessels became evident, then a bilander and a barquentine. One of the ships was definitely a trader, and soon decided she wanted no part of that brig on her port bow. Followed by the bilander, she headed for the defended port to larboard. The other ship was identified as either a large corvette or a small frigate. She put herself before the barquentine and ran out her guns.

Mister Prescott was agitated when he approached Phillips on the quarterdeck. "Sir, that frigate has eleven guns on a side. Do we want to take her on?"

"What would you guess their caliber, Mister Prescott? Perhaps eight pounders?"

"In my opinion Captain, I would guess eights, also. I wonder if that barquentine is armed also?"

"I doubt it, Mister Prescott. You will notice the frigate is signaling her, probably giving her instructions. I think he hopes we will believe she is armed."

The frigate took that moment to run up her colors, followed by firing a gun.

There was commotion on the barquentine's deck, and a tricolor rose up her mast. Phillips noted, "I think that fox is trying to fool us. There are not nearly enough men on her deck to be a French national ship, and she took too long to show her colors. I think she is following instructions from the frigate. Perhaps it is time to encourage this fellow, sir. Please run up the colors and show her our six pounders. Let us leave the carronades 'till later."

The six pounder long guns at bow and stern were run out. Phillips had most of the crew lie on the decks where they would be out of sight of the enemy.

It was now too late for any action against the trader or the bilander as both were entering the approaches to the port. The barquentine, perhaps still nervous about this brig with two guns protruding from her hull, reefed some canvas, and dropped away from the frigate a bit.

The frigate had turned to port a bit, and if the brig did nothing else, would soon be in a position to cross her bow and rake her. Before it came to that, Alert turned to port herself, and was then coming into long gun range of the frigate.

Both fired about the same time. Two six pounders from Alert against eleven eight pounders from the enemy. It was really too far for good shooting, but one of the balls from Alert struck the enemy just under her fore chains. In turn, two balls struck Alert. One punched a hole in her hull midships, causing no injuries. The other hit the starboard bulwarks behind which many of the crew were lying. Splinters cause a few significant wounds, and the men designated carried the injured below for the surgeon to practice his magic upon.

The combatants continued their approach, by now on slightly converging courses. The barquentine by now seemed to have given up her part in the play. She no longer answered signals from the frigate, and her ports had never opened.

Both fired again. Closer now, the two shots from Alert impacted the frigate, doing no obvious damage. Four of the balls from the enemy struck the brig. One ball made a notch on the bowsprit, for which the bosun's mate and a party of men rushed to make repairs. Another put a hole in the fore tops'l. The other two while striking the hull, did no important damage.

The first officer had his sextant in his hand, and periodically read off the angle to the enemy's main masthead. It was possible to convert that angle to the range if one knew the height of the masthead.

Mister Prescott read off his last estimate of the range, and Phillips decided they were close enough. He ordered the men behind the guns to stand up, and the ports to be opened. Probably, Phillips considered, the enemy had decided the brig was a simple trader, armed only by a few guns at her bow and stern.

The frigate had just fired her broadside which managed to destroy one of the six pounders and kill or wound half of the gun's crew.

The carronades, now uncovered, were already loaded, and the gun crew's blood was hot over the damage done to their brig and their mates. Mister Prescott ordered all the gun captains to take proper aim, and the midshipmen responsible for each gun section ran to each gun checking to ensure the order was followed.

These guns had sights the long guns did not, and it was possible to take greater care in aiming. Each carronade also had an adjusting screw to allow the gun captain to take particular care in the elevation adjustment.

Each gun captain had been warned, when the firing order came; that was not the signal to just jerk the firing lanyard. Instead, the gun captain was to determine the gun was aligned on the target, and was to take note of the state of the sea. Only when he was certain the ball would hit was he to fire.

The five starboard carronades erupted a few seconds after the order was given. The remaining six pounder long gun fired at the same time, with no obvious effect. Not so the carronades. The thirty two pound balls of iron smashed into the timbers of the enemy frigate with deadly effect. One smashed the ship's wheel, and her helmsmen were left lying on the deck.

The frigate, out of control until auxiliary steering might be rigged, began drifting stern first toward Alert. The light carronades were reloaded like lightning, with grape this time, and another broadside hammered home. Unable to respond with her stern presented right on Alert's beam, she was now nothing more than a target. Most of her officers were down, and her crew was not well worked up. The guns kept firing until the frigate crashed into Alert's quarter.

Phillips called for boarders, and the crew snatched half pikes, pistols, cutlasses and tomahawks from the arms chests. The fifty men delivered by the Impress Service back in Portsmouth, now proved their worth. Few were seamen, but many were familiar with rough and tumble conflicts on the waterfront. Even a peaceful solicitor's clerk could push a pike into an enemy's belly.

The frigate touching the brig stern first, swung around until she was lying beam to beam alongside Alert. A gun crew aboard her decided to fire one more shot for the 'Honor of the Flag'.

The ball smashed into the crowd of boarders on Alert, felling three of them instantly. Alert's men went out of control with rage, and poured over onto the deck of the frigate, slaughtering indiscriminately, even when her colors were dropped.

Phillips and Prescott had to go about knocking cutlasses aside with his own sword. One crazed landsman actually took a swipe at Phillips with a cutlass. Only the intervention of one of the Marines prevented the loss of the brig's captain.

CHAPTER TWENTY TWO

The frigate had suffered terrible losses, and the fight was now out of her crew. There was little resistance as they were herded below. Wilcox was left aboard the frigate with a crew of twenty seamen, and told to do his best to get the ship ready to sail. If Alert was not back by morning, he should try to make a British port.

Alert had some quick repairs done to her sails and rigging and set sail to see what could be done about the barquentine that was now nearly hull down to the north. Before the action, the enemy vessel was probably faster. Now, with the damage done to Alert's rigging, she certainly was. Phillips only pursued her in the hopes of meeting a ship of the Channel Fleet that might be patrolling in this area.

This was not to be though, and by morning there was no sign of her. They were now close to the shore of the new 'Kingdom of Holland', ruled by Napoleon's brother, Louis. Phillips missed Mister Wilcox, his sailing master that he had left in command of the prize. The waters in this area were treacherous, with shoals and sand bars. Phillips did not consider himself a pilot of this region's waters.

Alert began encountering fishing craft of all sizes. He did not regard them as prey, and left them alone. A sailing barge though, navigating from one sheltered bay to another, he brought to heel. This vessel was loaded to capacity with beef in barrels and sacks of biscuit, clearly provisions for Bonaparte's armies.

Alert was brought alongside and a few casks of beef were swayed over using tackle from the main yard. Some of the bags of biscuit were also loaded. Phillips considered this would give them a few days extra to patrol before it became necessary to re-supply. The extra hands he had aboard were rapidly consuming the rations loaded back at Portsmouth. When the supplies had been taken from the barge, she was cut loose, and two carronades were fired at her waterline at close range.

The barge was already low in the water, and it did not take long for her to go down. Alert came to the wind and resumed her patrol. Two of the barges former crewmen approached the bosun's mate who was about to stow them below as prisoners, and volunteered to serve in the Royal Navy. Mister Prescott gladly accepted the new recruits. They were already seamen, and both spoke adequate English

Sailing northward off the Frisian coast, another sail was seen coming toward them. This was a brig, much the same size as Alert. A privateer, rather than a National ship, she also had lighter armament. It was not unknown for some of these local craft to combine trading with privateering, doing a little of each. Often sailing with a light cargo, the craft would endeavor to snap up an unarmed trader when possible.

Of course, with a cargo, it was not possible to have many guns aboard. It would have been impossible to carry the numbers of men required to man them. Suspicious from the beginning, the private warship decided early on to stay away from this brig. Accordingly, she sheered away and made for the shoals along the shore.

Not wishing to trust his command to his knowledge of this coast, Phillips was ready to order his brig to come about and proceed out to sea.

Before the order left his mouth though, the chase slowed and came to a stop, her foremast going over the side. She had grounded on a sand bar. The situation now being altered, Alert's captain ordered the launch and cutter put in the water. With a sounding lead and pole in each boat, they pulled ahead of Alert surveying the bottom. Alert slowly crept her way through the twisting path the boats discovered for her.

The crew of the privateer, in a frenzy to get their brig afloat again, knocked a port in their stern and rigged a gun to fire from it. Seeing what was afoot, when he judged the brig to be in six pounder range, Phillips furled his canvas and slowed to a halt, with his larboard forward six pounder threatening the enemy. At the first shot from the brig, he dropped first his kedge anchor from the stern, then the bower.

The men at the brig's windlass wound in the excess slack, and the gun crew prepared to fire. The enemy was making poor practice with its stern mounted gun, but the crew knew it was a matter of time before a lucky shot connected.

Alert's gunner's mate got behind the gun and sighted down the barrel. The brig was almost stationary here in these coastal shallows, with no wind to speak of to stir up a chop. On Phillips quiet order, the gunner took one more sighting and pulled the lanyard.

From his location of the quarterdeck, Phillips ignored the explosion and the recoil of several tons of iron gun. For just the fleetest of moments he thought he saw the racing speck of the ball as it sped toward its target. The splash as it fell a few fathoms distance from the targets starboard beam was anticlimactic.

The gun crew immediately began its reload drill, as the enemy fired another round, this again was another miss. Alert's gun was levered over just the tiniest part of an inch and again the gunner took deliberate aim. This time the splash was just ahead of the enemy. The ball had apparently flown above her deck without actually hitting anything.

Mister Prescott spoke to the gunner, and then came back to the quarterdeck. "Sir, Hendricks does not want to disturb the elevation quoin, since the gun appears to be firing right over the target's deck.

He proposes he open the powder bag and take out a small amount of powder. I told him to do just that."

"That may be just the remedy, Mister Prescott. We will try another few shots to see what may be accomplished."

At the next shot, there was no splash evident, but one of the mids, peering through his glass, reported a hit. "Right beside the rudder sir. Port side."

Through his own glass, Phillips saw the ragged hole just above the waterline. Another shot missed to port, but the next one again sailed over the brigs deck, this time severing her main back stay. Since the enemy had earlier hoisted her main tops'l to try to lever herself from the sand, the mast with the cut stay slowly fell forward in a tangle.

With both masts down, the enemy's crew began going over the side into her boats and pulling toward shore. Alert pulled up her anchors and resumed her slow approach towards the target brig. As she neared, a trace of smoke appeared from a forward hatch.

Determined to make some profit from their labors of the day, Phillips collected a crew of volunteers and loaded into Alert's jolly boat. Leaving a vehemently protesting Lieutenant Prescott in command of Alert, Phillips set out for the target brig.

By now, smoke was billowing from the fore hatch. Phillips went aboard with his cox'n, ordering the rest of the crew to stand off. Seeing a few filled fire buckets near the privateer's abandoned guns, both he and Bates grabbed a pair and tossed the contents down the open hatch. They heard hissing as the seawater extinguished a bit of the fire. By the time the pair had emptied most of the available buckets, they had made obvious headway on the fire.

Calling the jolly boat over, he allowed most of the boat's crew on board and instructed the remaining oarsmen to return to Alert and bring over more people.

The smoke had thinned below deck on the prize, and Phillips and Bates went below with their buckets. The cargo in this section of the hull was sawn compass timber that had been splashed with a little oil and set afire. Fortunately, little oil had been used, and the timber, freshly sawn, was still green and not dry. Even with the accelerant, it had burned grudgingly, and the multiple buckets of water had slowed its spread.

As the additional people were brought aboard, more hands were put to extinguishing the remaining embers, and once the washdeck engine was found, the last of the fire was soon put out. The question now was, what to do with the vessel?

Phillips original thought had been to destroy her where she lay stranded, but that would be difficult. The flammable part of her cargo had already been drenched so it would be difficult to burn her. Aground, she could hardly be sunk. Examining her further, the hands found she had a secondary cargo of bulk wheat, still in good condition.

Much of her timber cargo had not been damaged and the compass timber, in demand for ship building purposes, would be of good value back home. This was wood that had grown into curved shapes while in the tree. It was needed for various parts of the ship that needed precurved timber.

Discussing the problem of the masts and rigging, his bosun's mate was sure he could get some spars erected to get her under sail. As far as the grounding was concerned, high tide would occur in a matter of a few hours, and it would be strange if they could not either float her off the bar, or at the least, kedge her off by setting an anchor in the channel and using the windlass to wind her off.

Alert had anchored close by the prize, and Phillips heard her lookout reporting the privateer's crew had landed on an offshore island, and were setting up camp.

Since the bosun's mate had matters under control aboard the prize, Phillips went back to Alert. He wondered why the privateer's crew had not continued on to the mainland. A glance at the chart showed the reason. Shoal waters extended for miles along the coast, making it difficult to travel even by small boat. The shore also was covered in extensive marsh. The only road was far inland.

It looked as though the fugitives might have to remain where they were until Alert left. As the captain meditated over his next action, he heard two crewman at work splicing some standing rigging injured in the recent action arguing. One man was certain they would never float the prize, and she would need to be abandoned, a pure loss of their prize money.

The other thought their 'young captain' might just be able to save the prize. The men had not realized Phillips was within earshot, and were shocked when he replied to their grousing. "Well, at least we can still collect some head money", he muttered.

CHAPTER TWENTY THREE

Phillips called for his Sergeant of Marines and the first officer. Explaining his plan to them, he ordered Mister Prescott to take charge of Alert and oversee the repairs of the prize, while he and some crewmen would take the boats and go see what could be done about gathering up the privateer crewmen on the offshore island. Loading the boat gun in to the launch, it and the cutter were pulled toward the island. After all, each enemy crewman was worth five pounds head money when surrendered at the dock.

It was necessary to back water once to avoid a section of shoal that neared the surface. At long musket shot range, the fugitives on the island tried a ranging shot with one of their Charleville muskets. This shot missed, but not the reply from the boat gun.

Port side oarsmen backing water, the boat turned in almost its own length. The gunner bent over the little twelve pounder carronade, rechecking the sights and tugged the lanyard. The gun belched smoke, fire and a cloud of musket balls at the people on shore. The boat had risen on a wavelet as the gun fired and much of the charge went high, but not all. Two of the privateersmen were struck by the balls and felled there on the beach.

Deciding a retreat was in order, the remainder took to their heels and fled over a rise to the other side of the tiny islet. Alert's men waded on shore confiscating supplies and equipment the others had brought. Many of their individual weapons had been left behind, and these were piled into the boats.

With no options left but surrender or attempt to wade to the mainland marshes, a man appeared waving a shirt on a length of driftwood.

He spoke a kind of English and it was decided the privateersmen would surrender and be sent to Britain. Their weapons were gathered and the rest of their belongings returned to them. The captives were left alone on the islet while Alert's crew went back to the brig and her stranded consort.

The bosun, in their absence, had made a start at getting the grounded brig, the Pluton ready to sail. Both main and fore masts had been broken, but their top masts were intact. The broken stubs were pulled from their seats on the keelson using a tripod of heavy timbers with a large block at the apex. Heavy line was connected to each stub in turn and led through the block to the brig's windlass. With the crew heaving on the windlass, each stub was pulled out. The former topmasts were stepped in place and wedged in tightly. Shrouds and fore and back stays were rigged to keep the spars upright.

The old rigging and sails had been badly damaged in the action, so simple lateen rigs were mounted.

The tide had risen enough so the bow was lifting slightly with each wavelet, although the stern was still embedded in the bottom. A kedge anchor was put in the launch and pulled out to water deep enough to float the brig. Dropped overboard, the cable was led through the hawse and nipped onto the messenger cable. With nearly the entire crew of Alert heaving, the Pluton was slowly twisted from her berth in the bottom and floated again. Not wishing to ground her again, the cutter and launch towed her out to deeper water, where a prize crew was put aboard, Midshipman Kearns in command.

The boats retrieved the stranded privateersmen on the islet, and they were put below in the prize. A large party of seamen were required to guard the prisoners and keep them below decks, so Phillips decided he must escort the Pluton to a British port. He suspected he might find himself in trouble for delaying his return to the Baltic, but decided his orders might just excuse his actions.

The pair set sail for Harwich Dockyard, Phillips deciding it might be better to remain away from Portsmouth until the return from the Baltic. The Pluton was a beast to control with her strange rig, but young Kearns learned her foibles and she made the best speed possible with her sails.

Anchoring in the harbor, Phillips was pulled ashore and reported to the Captain of the Port in his shoreside office. Phillips explained his unexpected entrance with a copy of his orders, telling the captain the capture of the frigate and now this brig had so depleted his crew, he was unable to go onward.

Captain Johnson was sympathetic, telling him they would give him back his prize crew, and see what other men might be found. Many commercial trading ships made port, but few King's ship fitted out here, so there were seamen aplenty who might be impressed, if they would not volunteer.

Phillips mentioned his absent master's mate who had taken the captured frigate into port, probably Portsmouth. Johnson was sympathetic but assured him the Admiralty would not stand for him waiting around to locate the man, then waiting for him to make his way here.

"I'll tell you what though, I have a young man who comes around now and then hoping for a berth. He was made master's mate last year, but his ship paid off and he has not been called for another. I know nothing about him, but I can send for him if you want to give him a try.

Master's Mate Hargrove approached a watering party from Alert on shore and begged for a ride to the brig. It seemed he did not have funds to hire a shore boat. He seemed to be an earnest, intelligent young man and Phillips took him on. His coat was worn to rags, and he had no hat so he would necessarily need to dress himself with slop clothing until he could draw on his pay.

The prisoners aboard Pluton were sent ashore to be put under control of a company of redcoats. Water and other supplies were loaded, and all that remained was to have their prize crew returned and attempt to locate some seamen to replace those sent off with the captured frigate.

It did not turn out to be necessary to resort to pressing seamen. Phillips had decided to allow some trusted hands ashore for a run. He was fairly sure they would return since he had gone over with them his estimates of their earnings to date with the prizes they had captured. If they did not desert, they would have several years pay just for their share of the prize money when Alert paid off. The lowliest landsman would have a sum of money that he could use to buy a small business.

When all the men returned from their run ashore, they brought with them a dozen new hands, recent arrivals from merchant ships. Having been landed, and spending all their money, they had succumbed to the tales of the riches to be earned under this captain of Alert.

Phillips welcomed them aboard and determined they could all be entered on the books as able seamen. After they all had made their marks, he asked, "Why did you men volunteer on a Royal Navy ship?"

"Well sir, it's like this", one seaman answered. "We hear you are not a hard horse captain, given to flogging at every turn of the watch. Then we hear you take plenty of prizes. Then too sir, in the Navy, there are plenty of men for each chore. A man need not rupture himself doing his job alone, like on some ships."

With all needs met, the signal requesting permission to proceed was hoisted. It flew without acknowledgement from shore for half a glass. The hands were at the windlass prepared to hoist the anchor and men were ready to set sail. Impatiently, Lieutenant Prescott worried about losing their tide. When the flagstaff on shore belatedly signaled 'Wait', Phillips sent the off watch below.

Finally, a boat was seen putting out from shore. A dapper midshipman came aboard with a sealed letter. Tearing it open impatiently, he found an order from Captain Johnson requiring him to wait on him in his shoreside office. Questioning the mid produced no intelligence, so he ordered the lad to take him ashore in his boat. He beckoned Mister Hargrove over. Hargrove now commanded the anchor watch while the brig was moored.

"Mister Hargrove, I am going ashore to see the port captain. When I am finished, I will signal for my boat. I would be glad if you would see the boat crew is properly turned out."

An aged seaman saw Phillips into the port captain's office. Captain Johnson had just told him good bye a few hours ago, now apparently he had some news to impart.

"Captain Phillips, your arrival here was reported earlier by telegraph. We just received a message by signal telegraph that you are required in Portsmouth. You should take Alert to sea as soon as possible, and proceed to Portsmouth, reporting to the port admiral. I have no further information to impart. You had better sail while you still have the tide."

As Phillips climbed aboard, he ordered all hands on deck to raise anchor and set sail. Mister Prescott was visibly curious but he could not satisfy the first officer's curiosity. Alert caught a good wind in the channel, and made short work of the passage.

When Alert anchored in Portsmouth Harbor, and made his number, it was only a short wait until he was signaled to report to the port admiral. By now, Phillips was certain he was about to lose his command for unnecessarily delaying his mission to the Baltic.

CHAPTER TWENTY FOUR

Phillips expected to be greeted by a grim admiral prepared to tear a strip off, but was surprised to be addressed cordially and have a glass of wine pressed into his hand.

After the amenities were over, Admiral Curtis got to the point. "Phillips, you are making quite a name for yourself. Taking a French National frigate as well as a privateer brig larger than your own command was quite a feat."

"However, it is now time to get down to work. Autumn is coming on and Admiral Saumarez must make certain dispositions with his fleet before the severe weather comes on. Admiralty needs intelligence on what those dispositions might be. The normal courier vessel never arrived as scheduled, so we fear she may have met with some misadventure.

Therefore, you will take the dispatches we have prepared and make the best of your way to the Baltic. You will find your leisurely cruise has been cancelled. It is imperative you reach Admiral Saumarez as soon as possible. You will avoid contact with the enemy so far as possible. Admiral Saumarez may well send you back immediately with his own dispatches. If you have no questions, you may return to your brig and set sail as soon as possible."

Phillips collected the dispatch case and returned to the ship. On board, Mister Prescott approached and requested leave for a few hours. It seemed a young lady he was fond of lived near the harbor, and he wished to pay her a visit.

"Mister Prescott, I would also like to visit a young lady. However, we are ordered to sail immediately."

Alert managed to stay away from any traffic that might threaten her up into the North Sea and into the Kattegat. She passed by Anholt Island and made her number, but continued on when no messages were hoisted. After entering the Baltic, she made it to the Gulf of Finland, where the near shore waters were starting to freeze in the frigid temperatures.

From a frigate patrolling outside the ice, he learned the Admiral Saumarez had taken the Victory to Carlscrona, where he was negotiating with the Swedes. Making her way there, Alert met the fleet as they were about to leave. Phillips was pulled over to the flagship in a near gale, and was happy to be handed a blanket and a hot grog in the great cabin.

After handing over his dispatches, Admiral Saumarez told him his brig would be needed to assist with the escort of the final trade convoy of the year as it made its way through the Belt and up the Swedish coast to the Skaw.

He was warned he must not show the British ensign in any fortified Swedish harbor. The Swedes were bound by treaty, after their defeat by the Russians, not to allow British warships or trading ships to enter any Swedish ports after the 15th of November. The ever courteous Swedes had assured the Admiral, since many of their ports especially the smaller ones, were not fortified, they could hardly prevent ships from entering to renew their provisions.

In order to avoid antagonizing their enemies though, it was hoped the British ships would avoid Swedish ports as much as possible.

The massive convoy set sail in mid-November. It was a cold and wet passage to The Downs, where Alert left the convoy and made her way back to Portsmouth. After saluting the flag and making her number, she received a signal for her captain to report to the flagship.

Admiral Curtis was indisposed, but the flag captain met with him and went over his reports. Learning Admiral Saumarez had left the Baltic, Phillips was told his brig would undoubtedly be put to use elsewhere. For now though, Alert would enter the dockyard to be surveyed and have any problems rectified, Phillips was told to go on leave until notified. Giving the address of his parent's town house in London, he got the last inside seat on the London coach and left Portsmouth.

The lights were burning when he arrived in the early evening on the following day. Additional servants were on duty, and when he introduced himself to the new butler, that individual assured him Captain Phillips would be notified immediately.

His father came rushing out of the game room and wrapped his son in his arms. "Son, I had no idea you were even in this hemisphere. How long have you before you sail again?"

Timothy assured his father his brig was in the dockyard and would probably remain there for the next two weeks. The pair went into the library where they spent the rest of the evening updating each other on their activities since last they met.

Phillips Senior was amazed at his son receiving his step to lieutenant's rank at so young an age, and marveled at his command of the brig. It was the next day before Tim told his father about the frigate Alert had taken earlier in the year.

"Son, I would not be surprised if you did not go up to commander. I know many a lieutenant who got that step for less."

CHAPTER TWENTY FIVE

Tim spent a few days with his father, then Phillips Senior left to board his frigate at the Nore. Tim coached out to Essex to visit his mother and sister. He had had a poor relationship with his mother in the past, but they had reconciled and spent a pleasant week together. One morning he drove her to the village and they had a pleasant time visiting the shops.

Another prize had been adjudicated, and Tim had money in his purse. He purchased a necklace for her at the goldsmith's shop. Ready now to go back to the estate, they walked to the coaching inn where they had left the coach and horses. Tim seated his mother in the carriage, then went to ask the hostler to bring the horses.

At this time, the London mail coach came clattering in. The mail bags were thrown off, a passenger boarded and off it went. The hostler had led out the team of matched bays and was hitching them to the carriage when the innkeeper came out with two letters.

"Both of these are for you, Lieutenant. Navy business, I think."

The first one was from the Master Superintendent of the Portsmouth dockyard. It informed Phillips that Alert was nearly ready and he should report to the dockyard as soon as possible.

The second had the Admiralty seal. It ordered Lieutenant Phillips to report forthwith to the Admiralty. Should he not do so, he was required to be prepared to offer his explanations as to why he should not be taken from the half-pay list.

The horses had by now been put to the carriage, and handing the letters to his mother, Tim popped his whip over them. There was some urgency. The coach would continue on to the next village, then turn and come back on the return leg to London. There would be some delay while the horses were changed, but then the coach would be off for London. Phillips needed to get his mother home, collect his belongings, and return to catch the London coach before it left.

Mrs. Phillips was handed down by the groom who had been chatting with one of the maids before the barn. His mother collected her purchases, and Tim ordered the groom onto the box, telling him they needed to make their best speed back into town.

The blown horses were pulled to a halt beside the newly arrived coach. There was time to pay the fare and to hoist Tim's sea chest aboard. With only two inside passengers, Tim was able to sit inside out of the cold and damp.

Since it was after dark when they reached London, Phillips spent the night in the town house and reported to the Admiralty early the next morning. He bought a cup of tea from a vendor, expecting to have to wait for hours, as was usually the lot of lieutenants. He expected an indignant Admiralty functionary had discovered he had never served in the wardroom of a warship and was about to set matters right.

Surprisingly, he had yet to take the first sip of his tea when a warder called out his name. He was led past a labyrinth of halls and offices, ending at one he remembered well.

Lord Viscount Eckersley greeted him warmly and asked him to sit. He had the reports Phillips had submitted after his voyages to the Baltic and read through them carefully. When finished, he put them down and stared at Phillips.

"Mister Phillips, I find myself in a quandary. It seems early this year you took a prize, a ship rigged corvette of sixteen guns. Your first officer of that time, Mister Wainright, brought her in. There was quite a stir in the press since the corvette had more guns than your brig. Of course your vessel was armed with thirty two pounder carronades, while the corvette had only eight pounders.

"Needless to say, the mob doesn't understand little facts like this and you and your first officer gained some notoriety. There was talk of promoting you both, but there were problems. You had been a lieutenant for only a watch, and it was hardly proper to promote such a youngster and, of course, it would hardly do to promote young Wainright over your head, with even less time holding a commission than yourself."

"The matter became more complex when Wainwright's cousin came into the picture. It seems he is the current Member for Milford and is curious why both you and his cousin have not been promoted. He reminds us dozens of other fine young officers have been elevated for similar feats."

"The matter has been handed over to me to investigate. I have been poring over your record and find you have been a very productive officer. Most officers your age have never seen an enemy ship, let alone captured one. You though, seem to do just that several times on every voyage."

"The thought occurs to me that your talents may be wasted on your little fourteen gun brig. With a larger ship you might be even more productive for the Royal Navy. Therefore, I have decided to give you a larger command."

"HMS Aurora is an eighteen gunned nine pounder sloop of war, just released from the Portsmouth dockyard. French built, she was taken two years ago. Much battered, it has taken this long for her to be put back together. She is a little elderly, but I am told she has fine lines and should be a swift sailer."

Phillips was astonished with the news. "Milord, I wonder about a letter that arrived in the post yesterday bidding me to return to Portsmouth to take Alert from the dockyard."

"Well Phillips, if you would rather have the brig instead of the sloop…"

"Sir, I am most happy to be given the sloop. I was just curious about receiving two letters in the same post. One calling me to return to Alert. The other calling me here."

The viscount explained, "Apparently the dockyard has not kept up their correspondence. They were told Mister Wainright would be taking command. Because of political pressure, I have decided to assign Alert to him to see what he can do with her. I was reluctant to do so, but should he fail with the command, there is a simple remedy. We can either put him on the beach or place him in the wardroom of a line-of-battle ship where he can learn more of his profession."

"I should probably tell you, that same remedy applies to you. Should you fail to perform adequately, you may be sent ashore on the half-pay list."

"Commander Phillips, I am told your new command will not be ready for a matter of a few weeks. I am sure you wish to post down to look her over, but I hope you have time to attend a little soirée my good wife is having tomorrow evening. The delightful Miss Hilda you brought to us will be there as my wife's guest."

With much of the day before him yet, Timothy repaired to a tailor he had heard recommended.

The man specialized in military and naval uniforms and was reputed to be able to produce one rapidly. If necessary, he supposed he could go to the house and borrow one of his father's old coats, merely needing to remove the epaulette from the right shoulder.

However, he knew his father's coats would be a loose fit on his body. As it happened, the tailor had a coat he had started to make for another officer who had left London before taking delivery. The tailor was glad to turn a potential loss into profit and Phillips was clad in his new coat when he went to the party.

CHAPTER TWENTY SIX

Hilda was a vision in her gown and young officers were in line to dance with her. Never having mastered that art, Phillips remained on the sidelines watching. As he began thinking of an excuse to leave, a familiar touch startled him. Susanne Wilder was standing by his side, looking ravishing as usual.

Bored and restless, he got into conversation with her. After a few moments, he wondered if he had misjudged her. She was intelligent, charming and witty, not at all the dominating young woman he had thought.

Soon, she had her hand on his arm listening raptly as he explained the tactics of his last battle. She was very impressed with his promotion, wondering if he could be the youngest man to be promoted to commander.

The pair was intently engaged in conversation, hardly aware of anything around them. The current dance ended, and Hilda's partner left her on the floor by the couple to get something to drink. Hilda, only a few feet away from Timothy, started to approach him, but saw he was busily engaged in conversation with Susanne.

Giving a little sniff, she turned to the next man to approach her, and as the musicians started to play, she danced off with her new partner.

When it was time to post down to Portsmouth, he left a message at the door of Viscount Eckersley's home for Hilda. He expressed his regret at not being able to spend time with her. He had called multiple times while in London, but it always seemed she was 'indisposed'.

He assured her he would write, and asked that she reply. With Susanne, there were no difficulties. She had been available any time he came around to her rooms, and assured him she would answer all his letters.

Getting back into the naval atmosphere in Portsmouth was a relief. He found it had been a strain attempting futilely to maintain good relations with one woman while failing to keep another woman at arm's length. It was better to be back in an atmosphere he was familiar with.

Before he went near HMS Aurora, he stopped by Alert. Wainright was there and he had Phillips piped aboard. There were still some familiar faces among the crew, but many had been drafted to other ships and replaced with the dregs of the press.

After spending an hour reminiscing about times past, Phillips took his departure. He had engaged the crew of the shore boat for the full day and they were waiting for him when he left Alert.

The cox'n knew just where Aurora lay, and took him directly there. He was prepared to love her despite her faults, but the ship did give him pause. The ship had fine lines as he had been told, but she was drab. Not a ha'penny had been expended on paint, her standing rigging was a horror, and her deck was covered with trash left over from her fitting out. Her standing officers that had remained aboard during her years in ordinary had all been drafted away onto other ships. The replacements had not yet reported and the only soul on board was an ancient watchman.

Not wasting a moment, Phillips had the boat take him to the dockyard where he located the superintendent's office. He walked right in, disturbing three men drinking rum in the middle of the day. When one protested, he offered to visit Admiral Curtis and invite him to inspect Aurora which was reputed to be nearly ready to sail.

Seeing the official beginning to dig in his heels, Phillips changed course. He told them he realized that it was expensive these days to get things done, and sometimes the government did not allow sufficient funds.

He assured him that he was prepared to write out a note of hand for a significant sum if he could expect to have the ship looking as it should within a week's time. After some negotiation an amount was agreed upon, and Phillips handed over a portion of the money. He assured the official he would have more funds to hand over when he saw the results from this money.

The standing officers began coming in ones and twos. With them came the materials each was responsible for. When the first few men came aboard, the purser was able to supply slop clothing to those who needed it, and the cook had his salt pork, beef and peas to feed them. When the new first officer reported aboard, Phillips asked Lieutenant MacDonald to draw the few crewmembers up before the quarterdeck and read the orders giving him the command of the ship.

This act officially confirmed his command and he began earning his pay of 20 pounds per lunar month from that moment. As men began coming aboard, the ship became crowded, with the dockyard workers underfoot. The ship was coming together. A dozen seamen came aboard from a fishing boat one night. They had heard of the prize money this captain had earned for his previous crews and wanted some of that themselves.

In order to escape the press, the men had not dared to come through the dockyard so had persuaded the captain of a drifter to bring them to the sloop.

As volunteers, Phillips decided he could use them for recruiting duty. He hired a wagon and team to pull the seamen around outlying towns where the petty officer in charge would set up office in the pub and pay for the drinks for prospective recruits while the seamen would talk about their seagoing experiences. They gathered no seamen in these country towns, but did garner a number of itinerant farm laborers who wished more excitement in their lives as well as a steadier income.

By the time the draft of men from the Impress Service came aboard, Aurora's captain thought he was as prepared as most captains were at the beginning of their voyage.

Phillips had received no sailing order yet and had no idea of where the sloop might be destined. A welcome surprise came one winter day. A chaise pulled up on the quay opposite their mooring. A man and woman got out and began waving at the ship. Mister Atkins commanding the anchor watch thought this warranted calling the captain. Phillips came out on deck and leveled his glass. The two were Hans Kofoed and his sister Hilda.

The trio had a most pleasant afternoon. For a day in the middle of winter, the sky was clear, and it was possible, at least for a glass or so, to sit on the quarterdeck in deck chairs.

When Phillips saw Hilda shivering though, he took them into his cabin. After some conversation, Hans discreetly withdrew, saying he wished to see the difference between this ship and Alert.

Hilda abruptly apologized for ignoring him at the dance while Phillips insisted he was at fault for spending so much time with Susanne. It was decided the two would correspond while he was at sea on the forthcoming voyage.

When Hans came back, he remarked how much colder it had become in the last hour. He thought they should get the horses back to the barn. Phillips apologized to Hilda once more as she went through the entry port to climb down into the boat. Their boat had no sooner reached shore when the flagship flew a signal for Aurora to send an officer.

When the boat returned, Mister MacDonald took it to the flag. When he returned he handed a sailcloth wrapped packet to his captain. Captain Phillips took it into his cabin and opened it. Inside were the expected sailing orders and another wrapped packet. The sailing orders merely ordered the sloop to put to sea and to proceed to a position which Phillips knew to be off Land's End, where he was required to open the second packet.

Phillips went out on deck and called Mister MacDonald away from his task of inspecting the stowage of the hold. Actually, this was a task for their master's mate, but this young man had only recently been elevated to that height, and Phillips wanted to be sure the tiers of beef and pork casks below did not suddenly shift in bad weather.

When MacDonald reported to the quarterdeck, Phillips handed him the orders without a word. After reading them through, the first officer looked at him questioningly. Not knowing himself what the mystery was about himself, Phillips speculated. "Perhaps their lordships wish us to do something they would rather not let others know about. In any event, we will know soon enough."

CHAPTER TWENTY SEVEN

HMS Aurora had more than her share of inept landsmen, now occupied mostly in puking over the lee rail, now that the ship was beating to windward out in the channel. She did have just enough seamen to sail her though and she was heading for her designated position called for in her orders. It took her a few days to reach that position and Phillips and his first officer kept the hands busy with sail and gun drill.

At first, many of the landsmen seemed convinced they could not possibly do the tasks that were demanded of them, but bosun's mates, equipped with knotted ropes ends, did their best to convince them otherwise. Men gibbering with fear were driven willy-nilly up the masts then back down until they realized they could actually do this.

Gun drill was much the same. Aurora was a miniature frigate, with her ship-rig and her eighteen nine pounder guns. She carried 120 crewmembers, many of them landsmen. 36 men were needed to man the guns of one side, but many of these did not have to be trained seamen.

In addition to simply running the guns in and out, all members had to learn their various duties in an engagement. It was hard, physically exhausting work for men who may not have been in their best condition. One group of 'quota men', men who had been foisted upon the ship from local counties, decided they would no longer do this work.

Most captains would at a minimum flog the lights out of the culprits, if they were not bound over for court martial. Either course would ruin any man so punished, whether being crippled by the 'cat' or hung. Captain Phillips adopted a different course. Those men not wishing to take part in the training were placed below at the pumps and required to pump ship while their mates were exercising the guns. Aurora was an old and 'wet' ship, required to pump ship every day.

Those not doing their fair share at the pump handle would have a bosun's mate stationed behind to 'encourage' the slacker. Probably the best encouragement to the prospective gunners was the issue of grog which was served out after the training session ended. Of course, those men manning the pumps as punishment did not receive their issue.

While no one would say the sloop-of-war had a well-trained crew by the time she reached her station off Land's End, she was at least as capable as many other King's ships putting to sea. Her men could now make and handle sail without inordinate confusion and fire a broadside from one side. Mister McDonald, her first officer, was definitely not satisfied, but assured his captain he would soon get the crew up to standard.

On reaching the position specified in their orders, Phillips invited MacDonald into his cabin and had his servant open a bottle of Madeira. While he was doing so, Phillips took out of his desk the sealed packet he had received before sailing.

Opening it with his penknife, he read the document inside then handed it to his first officer. MacDonald read the cramped handwriting with some difficulty then wondered.

"We're to rendezvous with a merchant vessel flying a 'Blue Peter" here and take a passenger on board. He will identify himself as Pierre Longchamps and will carry a paper with a copy of a single sentence of these instructions. He will give us the details of the task we are to perform, and will accompany us on our mission. It all sounds very mysterious."

Phillips mulled over the matter. "I do not care for the idea I must blindly follow the instructions of some French stranger. However, we will give it a try. If this person tells us we must perform some task that will unduly endanger the ship or crew, we may talk more about this. In the meantime we will do as our orders instruct."

Aurora stood back and forth on the line of latitude that covered the ordered position. After a week of this, MacDonald was all for leaving and announcing the failure of the mission. Phillips though, thought differently. "I realize this is beginning to look like a wild goose chase but it does give us the time to work up our crew."

Indeed, the crew was becoming more proficient every day. Before leaving port, Phillips had purchased a limited amount of powder and shot, which he now permitted the better gun crews to fire sparingly, as a reward for their good efforts. One morning, Aurora left her line of latitude to approach the shore where his master's mate knew of good holding ground. There, they anchored, and practiced placing a spring on the cable and using that to veer the ship around to present her broadside in different directions.

Then, while anchored in reasonably calm waters, the boat crews were exercised. After a few hours at the oars, the launch and cutter crews tried their hand at boarding the sloop. It was a tired crew that hoisted anchor and set sail again for their rendezvous position. They were in a happy mood, since the captain had broken out a cask of privately purchased rum and issued an extra grog ration that evening as well as announcing a hornpipe competition.

While only the seamen were familiar with hornpipe dancing, there were men on board from rural areas who were expert in the country dances of their area, and were happy to demonstrate their expertise. It was a satisfied crew that reached their patrol position late that evening.

Next morning, Phillips decided another reward was in order. After the decks had been sanded down and flogged dry, he announced a 'Make and Mend' day. On this day there would be no training or unnecessary labor. Of course, the masthead would still have a lookout posted, and crew would be handy if it were necessary to trim sail, but the others were free to take a place on deck and use the time to repair or sew clothing, carve trinkets or just yarn with their messmates.

In the afternoon Phillips, pacing fore and aft along the windward quarterdeck rail, had just noted to himself how well the crew was coming along, when the masthead lookout hailed. "Sail in sight off the port quarter, hull down."

Everyone on the quarterdeck with access to a glass raised it to see what he could. Phillips was no exception but could see nothing on the horizon. Beckoning over the Master's Mate standing by the helm, Phillips said, "Mister Horton, I would be pleased if yon put the ship about. I would like to close that sail."

Since the lookout was at the highest elevation on the ship, he was able to see objects before other members of the ship's crew.

The ship, having just steadied on its new course, was alerted when the lookout shouted the sail appeared to be a brig that was now hull up. A moment later, MacDonald, with his highest quality glass, announced he had the brig in sight. By leaning against the mizzen to steady himself, Phillips was able to catch sight of the stranger himself. Aurora was flying her ensign and the commissioning pennant at the time of sighting. Phillips ordered her number flown, just in case this vessel had a copy of the Royal Navy's signal book aboard with someone to decipher the signal flags.

The brig, when it finally approached, proved to be a dowdy trading craft, her hull innocent of paint, and her sails composed of more patches than whole sailcloth. The only flag she wore was a blue signal flag with a white square in the center, a 'Blue Peter', normally the signal used to indicate a ship was ready to leave port.

As the brig heaved to, a skiff was pulled forward from where it had been towing astern, and a crew tumbled into it. Upon reaching Aurora's port side. A short man clad in ragged fisherman's garb clambered aboard. There had been no reply to the midshipman's hail so the Royal Marine sergeant had a guard stationed at the entry port in case the individual required either a salute or arrest.

Curious, Phillips wandered over to the port while the man made his way up the battens. Stepping on deck. The fellow was a short man, barely five feet tall. He had an impressive girth, and Phillips imagined the man had a hard time pushing away from the dinner table.

Seeing Phillips waiting before him, he doffed his ragged hat and made a bow. "Sir, I am Major

Hendricks, seconded from Horse Guards. I have a bit of paper I am to show you."

From the lining of his cap Hendricks produced a scrap of paper and extended it to Phillips. "Turn about is fair play, Captain. Would you be so kind to show me a copy of your secret orders?"

Phillips examined the paper. To the best of his recollection, the words scribbled on the paper in almost indecipherable handwriting matched the wording of one of the sentences of his orders. "Come into my office Major, and I will produce my papers."

Adjourning to the captain's day cabin and the requisite wine poured, Major Hendricks looked significantly at the servant and said, "It would be better if no one overheard us, Captain."

Phillips dismissed the servant and shouted for the sentry outside his door. "Private Fletcher, I want you to take up your post out of earshot. Up on deck would be the best place until I am finished with this gentleman.

The reluctant Royal Marine left the area, and Major Hendricks got down to business. "Of course Captain, you are aware of the events that brought the Spaniards into alliance with us. I am sure you are aware of the rescue of La Romana Division from the clutches of Napoleon in Danish waters by ships of the Baltic Fleet when Admiral Richard Keats had the Fleet?"

"As it happens, we have a similar situation awaiting us today. After the rescued Spanish troops were loaded aboard the British transports and sailed away from Danish waters, a Division made up of troops stationed in Swedish Pomerania from such conquered Italian nations as Genoa, Venice and the Papal States heard the news and began agitating for freedom themselves."

"General Bernadotte commanding French forces in the area, in an effort to contain the situation ordered the entire unit to several Danish islands off the coast of Jutland."

"I am told they do not care for the climate so far north of Italy. An agent of the British government managed to reach Nakskov on the island of Lolland where General Pietro Cadorno, the commander of the Italian troops was headquartered. The agent came to a preliminary agreement with the second in command of the division, General Cesari Falcone, who wishes to return to Italy. At this time, of course, this would mean Sicily which is protected by the Royal Navy. We will attempt to furnish the necessary shipping to facilitate the move. Your part in the program is to proceed to the Baltic, confer with Admiral Saumarez and give him some dispatches I have concerning the matter."

"Should he concur, you may find yourself in the position of making contact with the Cadorno troops as a representative of the Navy. I will accompany you and may go ashore to make initial contact. I speak fluent Italian as well as German and will portray myself as an itinerate peddler of cigars. I have a large supply of Cuban cigars aboard the merchantman."

Phillips digested this information. "Very well major. I will find you a place to rest your head tonight. In the meantime, have you anything aboard the merchantman you need?"

"As it happens I do, Captain. I have some parcels in the other ship which I must not be parted from, as well as the cigars, of course."

CHAPTER TWENTY EIGHT

While Major Hendricks was discussing the transfer of his kit aboard the merchantman, Phillips called the carpenter to his cabin. Chips agreed he could put up a partition in the sleeping cabin itself to accommodate another resident. He did not know what to do about the bed, though. Phillips had a hanging bed, suspended from lines to the overhead.

He could make another frame, but did not know what to do about a mattress or bedding. Phillips waved him off. He would let the major use his own bed, and sling a hammock for himself.

With the envoy's belongings aboard, Aurora set sail for the Skaw. The voyage went well apart from Phillips re-introduction to the hammock. He had not cared for it as a midshipman, and cared less now as a captain. Aurora sailed north well away from the continental coast, but as they were nearing Jutland, the lookout spotted sails ahead. It took a glass before they were near enough to identify.

One was a ship-rigged vessel similar to their own, two others were a different breed. One was a craft Lieutenant MacDonald called a hoecker, a small, bluff bowed merchant craft. The other was a schooner. The trio was headed their way and came quite near before someone woke up. Abruptly, the brig and hoecker turned to port and headed for

Hamburg, which lay some leagues to the leeward. The ship, which soon was identified as a corvette, continued toward them.

Phillips would rather have not been placed in this situation. While he was not hampered with orders requiring him from combat, he knew well if something went awry when the pair of equally matched ships engaged, he could be severely admonished. Seeing Major Hendricks standing in the bows watching the oncoming corvette, he dispatched a midshipman to ask the envoy to go below.

Instead, the major came storming aft, protesting loudly. "I am a military officer and I should not be required to hide below like some frightened fool. You would besmirch my honor, Sir!"

Knowing he was on the verge of being called out by this hothead, Phillips agreed to let him stay on deck, much against his will. Tending to ship's business he lost track of Hendricks for a time, until the officer appeared on the quarterdeck with one of the spare muskets. The bayonet was fixed and altogether the weapon was longer than he was tall.

As the ships neared, Phillips tried the old trick of turning across the opponents bow in order to gain position for a raking broadside. The enemy turned with him and they ended up beam to beam, a musket shot apart. The gunners had been warned they were to fire only when they had the target ship in their sights, so Phillips had no qualms about ordering, "You may fire when ready."

The guns began thundering in singles and pairs as they came on target. The enemy commander believed in firing by broadside, and thus found herself struck by several of the nine pound balls before she deigned to reply. The corvette was armed similarly to Aurora, with nine of the French eight pound guns firing almost simultaneously. The French pound was a bit heavier than the English weight, so the two types of guns were roughly similar in caliber.

Since the French gunners were firing by order of their captain, and since some of the guns were aimed high to impact their rigging, few rounds hit the hull. Every one of Aurora's balls had struck the target, and now there appeared to be two empty gun ports in the corvettes hull. While a few of Aurora's guns were not being served quite as fast as Philips would have liked, by and lrge, they were firing and reloading faster than the enemy.

The enemy was trying to edge closer to Aurora, but when Phillips saw the number of boarding pikes appearing over the rail of the enemy, indicating a horde of boarders, he sheared off to avoid coming on board. A word to the messenger midshipman by his side sent that lad to warn the gunners to reload with grape. A few moments later, when the grape loaded guns fired, the number of healthy enemy boarders decreased dramatically.

The gunners were getting their rhythm now and despite the men growing tired, the guns were being fired faster now. As Phillips watched the enemy, he thought their gunners were using the old style linstocks, rather than the modern flintlocks. The linstock held a length of smoldering slowmatch, which the gunner applied to the touch hole to fire the gun. This required the gunner to stand to one side so the gun would not crush him when it recoiled. Standing in this manner made it difficult to take careful aim.

The British gunners however, could stand at a distance behind their guns, giving orders to the gun crews to adjust the aim of the weapon. When ready to fire, he could aim down the barrel and pull the lanyard to fire when the gun was on target. The gun's breach ropes would stop the recoiling gun before it reached his body.

It was evident the enemy was firing slower, and were not always hitting. As he watched number four gun fire, he saw the muzzle of an enemy's gun that had just been run out to fire, suddenly vanish. Number four gun's ball had struck the muzzle of the enemy weapon and dismounted it.

Now, the enemy mizzen had been struck and he saw a long split beginning to travel in the big spar. The corvette's captain saw it too, and men were called away from the guns to go aloft to reduce sail. A shot sounding behind him revealed Major Hendricks with his smoking musket. "Got the bastard, gloated the officer. He was apparently taking potshots of the enemy's crew as they worked above the decks.

The enemy did get the mizzen sails off and were able to save the mast, but now Aurora sailed right ahead and started the turn across the bow of the now slower ship. As Aurora was poised to loose her raking broadside down the length of the enemy ship, her tricolor came down with a rush.

Both Phillips and MacDonald shouted "Cease fire!", but a few frenzied gun crew sent their balls rocketing down the length of the corvette. Everyone else refrained, and remained poised to resume their fire a second's notice.

The launch was pulled up from its position trailing astern and Royal Marines and seamen loaded aboard. Mister MacDonald accompanied them and took the ship's surrender.

The corvette's crew was immediately ordered below, while it's officers, after accepting parole, were sent to their own wardroom. The enemy's small arms, now scattered on deck, were unceremoniously thrown over the side.

With the prize under control, Phillips looked about for the two merchant craft the corvette had been escorting. The schooner had started for shore but had changed her mind and was sailing west, closely into the wind.

Knowing she could sail closer to the wind than he could in the square-rigged Alert, he let her go, instead concentrating on the hoecker. This was an unattractive, bluff bowed craft, fat and slow. It was headed for the mainland, but unless there was a mishap with Aurora's rigging, it was unlikely she would make it.

CHAPTER TWENTY NINE

There was no mishap and the surging sloop-of-war came alongside just before the pair came in range of the shoreside battery the hoecker was heading for. Seeing the sloop's broadside aimed at her diminutive hull, the hoecker let fly her sheets and she wallowed to a halt. Another prize crew was hurriedly put aboard her, commanded by his master's mate, a young man he hated to lose. Beating back against the wind to the prize corvette, they had a pair of pleasant surprises.

First, it seemed the corvette had had an encounter with a British dispatch cutter a few days before. The cutter had been so damaged during the action the French had burned her afterward, taking her crew on board. This crew had now been set free, from the tiny storage space where they had been confined during the action. He found he now had a Royal Navy lieutenant in his hands, formerly captain of the Badger; with a master's mate and twenty seamen.

Additionally, the prize hoecker was found to have a cargo of scrap brass and bronze, some of it old worn out guns while the remainder proved to be bronze church bells looted by the conquering French army. This was a valuable cargo indeed and the proceeds from its sale would bring a tidy sum to the captain and crew.

Lieutenant Wheeler, the former commander of the dispatch cutter, had been struck in the arm by a large splinter during the action but the French had given him proper care. He assured his rescuers that he could assume the duties of second in command of Aurora.

Half of the extra men were sent to the prizes to help man them and the voyage to the Skaw was resumed. Phillips had been tempted to send his prizes back to Britain, but both were seaworthy and adequately manned now, so he decided to take them to the rendezvous with the Baltic Fleet.

The remainder of the voyage through the Skagerrak and Kattegat were without incident, although the little fleet did visit the island of Anholt in the Kattegat. This had formerly had a light to warn mariners of the dangerous rocks and shallows nearby. When the Danes extinguished that light with the commencement of hostilities, it was captured and occupied by British forces to ensure its light was kept burning for the protection of British trade and the Baltic Fleet. While exchanging gossip with the garrison commander there, Phillips mentioned his crewmen would be glad to get some fresh meat to provide a change from the incessant salt beef and pork.

A few hours later, a boat appeared on Aurora's beam and a weather-beaten man wearing fisherman's garb stepped aboard. Speaking very broken English, he said he had fish for sale, as well as a few sheep. On an earlier visit, Phillip's vessel had delivered some much needed cattle to the island since the garrison had difficulty in procuring food. Now though, some ambitious Swedes were supplying livestock to the islands inhabitants and garrison.

Fish was not the crew's favorite food, but Phillips bought the man's catch as well as six sheep. This was a Friday, a banyan day, when ordinarily no meat would be served to the crew. Since the captain had purchased the fish with his own funds, he felt justified in substituting the ancient, crumbling purser issued cheese with the fresh cod.

The sheep were dispatched on the next Wednesday, the next banyan day. Phillips shared one beast with the wardroom while the others went to the ship's cook to serve to the crew.

In a final discussion with the garrison commander, Captain Crawford informed him to be careful passing Zealand by way of the Oresund, the narrow waterway separating the Danish island of Zeeland from the Swedish mainland. He assured Phillips the Danish gunners on the Zealand batteries were most active and proficient. This narrow strait between the Danish Saltholm Island and the Swedish shore was especially dangerous.

Phillips, of course, had sailed this route before and felt he could rely on his own experience. The three vessel dallied at sea until conditions were right. With an overcast sky and minimal moonlight and a fresh breeze on her quarter, Aurora and her little fleet set course through the strait, passing as close to the Swedish mainland as was possible, showing no lights. No one took notice, and they passed safely into the Baltic.

With his vessels in a line abreast formation, spaced so they could just make out their neighbor's signals, they made their way up the Baltic. Eventually, they spoke a British Baltic trading brig who informed them of the probable location of the fleet.

Admiral Saumarez was still on HMS Victory and was happy to obtain news from the Admiralty as well as mail from home. Phillips was entertained by the flag captain while the Admiral and his clerk pored over the official dispatches and read his mail.

It was an hour before Phillips and Major Hendricks was told to report to the Admiral. Phillips and the admiral had of course met earlier on a previous voyage to the Baltic and Saumarez reminded Phillips of the event, commending him for his promotion and the new ship.

The men, over cigars furnished by Hendricks and brandy by the admiral, began discussing the proposed reconnaissance. From reports of different agents, Admiral Saumarez reported the two generals of the Italian Legion were at odds with each other. General Cadorno at Nakskov on the island of Lolland, was an admirer of Bonaparte, while Falcone despised the man, secretly of course.

Falcone had removed to Rodbyhavn, miles to the south, on the coast. Falcone had many of the troops with him, while Cadorno kept the artillery and cavalry close by. Saumarez had decided to send an emissary to Falcone to inquire if he might wish to be removed from Lolland with his troops and taken to Sicily.

Admiral Saumarez decided the major would be the emissary, while Phillips would carry him there. The admiral hoped Falcone could be persuaded to bring his troops in from the hinterlands, where they were barracked, into Rodbyhavn where transports could take them aboard.

Aurora set sail the next morning, carrying Hendricks' cigars as well as cases of wines 'borrowed' from the wardrooms of the fleet. Admiral Saumarez felt the Italian officers might appreciate some entertaining and thus be more reluctant to turn them in to Bonaparte's agents. A large purse of guineas went along, just in case gold might be a motivating factor.

The prize corvette captured earlier by Phillips accompanied them. La Rochelle had been given a hurried survey and repair and manned by seamen drafted from other ships of the fleet. Admiral Saumarez bought her into the Royal Navy and Mister MacDonald was given his step and promoted to Commander. The captured seamen, many of which were Dutch or German, were asked if they would like to serve in the Royal Navy instead of going to the prison hulks. Most of the latter seamen volunteered, while nearly all of the French indignantly refused. The volunteers were distributed around the fleet as needed.

HMS Aurora, accompanied by HMS La Rochelle made their way to Lolland. The weather took a turn for the worse during the voyage and both ships were severely hampered by the sky being obscured. Unable to navigate by sights of the sun or stars, they were obliged to manage by dead-reckoning and attempting to fix their position by use of chart and lead line.

A group of Danish fishing boats out for cod one dreary morning gave them the first accurate information of their location they had had in days. Phillips pressed one of Saumarez' guineas upon the reluctant fishermen and were soon at their destination.

Anchoring far enough off-shore that their identities would not be apparent, Major Hendricks prepared to go ashore in the longboat. He dressed in his ragged peddler's clothing, and wore a discarded French leather pack on his back, full of Spanish cigars.

A few crewmen, dressed in old fisherman's clothing took the boat in under sail early in the morning and dropped Hendricks off at the quay, to the amazement of half a dozen locals. With the emissary clear of the boat, it sailed back to Aurora.

The ships stood out to sea, occasionally sending the longboat in to see if there was any sight of the major. On the third day, the longboat's crew reported there was an old shirt draped on a rock at the shore, as previously arranged, but the Major was not in sight. The two sloops again approached the land later in the day, and this time a few men were sitting at a fire on the beach by the signal.

This time Phillips, accompanied by a file of Royal Marines dressed in slop clothing with their muskets out of sight, approached in the boat. Hendricks was among the group at the fire and did not appear to be under restraint. Phillips went on shore and approached the men. Hendricks gave a brief report in front of his companions, indicating all was well and General Falcone wished to meet with Captain Phillips.

In due course, a worn carriage was produced. Drawn by four small, undernourished horses, Phillips, Hendricks and a pair of Italian officers were carried inland to the estate where General Falcone resided.

Falcone spoke no English, so Hendricks did the translating. Over clouds of cigar smoke and glasses of rough wine, the men came to an agreement. It would be necessary for the transports to be close at hand before Falcone could make a move. General Cadorno was at most a day's march away, and could arrive with guns and horse if the embarkation took too long.

Cadorno would not consider going over to the English and had threatened to report Falcone for even discussing the matter. Even so, Falcone thought he could extricate the single battalion of infantry that were with Cadorno. It was known that Cadorno's favorite mistress was away visiting her mother in Copenhagen. It was thought if the embarkation could be delayed until the mistress returned, Cadorno might be otherwise occupied and might not notice the activity until it was too late.

Thus, orders would be sent to the commander of the infantry battalion that was providing guard services at the estate. These orders would put the officer on notice to have the battalion report to the harbor at Rodbyhavn on a date in the future that would be decided later. The battalion would join the remainder of the division and prepare to defend the beach against a mock invasion.

Of course General Cadorno would soon hear of this, mistress or no and rush to Rodbyhavn himself, probably with the artillery and cavalry. If the transports were not close by prepared to embark the troops, there could well be a bloodbath.

Philips wondered what number and caliber of guns might be present. After a brief consultation, Hendricks reported, "The Italian Division has perhaps a dozen guns, although the condition of the carriages and lack of horses might prevent some of them from coming. The guns would mostly be what we would call four pounders, with a pair of nines."

This relieved Phillips mind. He had more guns than the soldiers did and he could do more harm to their troops than they could do to him, especially if the guns were in the open and not behind any type of fortification. The general wanted Phillips to leave an officer as hostage while he reported back to Admiral Saumarez to fetch the transports.

This idea was flatly turned down. Then Phillips offered to remain with Aurora while La Rochelle went back to alert the transports. This Falcone accepted. It was felt he was mainly interested in a vehicle of escape for himself in case the plot fell through and he learned General Cadorno was on his way to arrest him.

La Rochelle set sail that afternoon to fetch the transports that evening, and it was nearly two weeks before she returned with a message the transports were right behind. Falcone was almost gibbering with fear. The mistress had returned early and Cadorno and his Miss Andersen had had a spat and were no longer living together. Cadorno now had plenty of time to see to his troops and had actually spent a few days in Rodbyhavn.

Falcone was sure Cadorno suspected him and was just toying with him before placing him under arrest. Phillips was adamant he should make a strong attempt to extricate all of the Italian soldiers he possibly could, despite the antagonisms of the senior officer.

With the transports offshore, and the boats ready to begin ferrying troops, Phillips was at Falcone's headquarters trying to urge the general to get a move on. Falcone had somehow come to the conclusion he might be better off if he were to denounce the extraction and try to make peace with Cadorno.

Phillips was totally disgusted with the dithering fool. His ships were in dangerous waters, and a sudden storm could cause dreadful damage. Suddenly, an Italian aide to General Falcone burst through the door and began an outburst of rapid Italian. He turned to Hendricks for a translation. The major's face was ashen.

"I'm afraid it may be over, Captain. Cadorno has just ridden up with a party of officers. Falcone will give up, as sure as fate"

"Can we try to take this port, Major?"

"Falcone could. He has enough men, he just doesn't have the courage. "

With everyone in the room in a state of panic, Phillips began to think he needed a weapon with more authority than his sword. From a startled Italian soldier he snatched a long barreled musket, with a bayonet twisted onto the muzzle. At the same moment the door burst open and a corpulent, middle-aged man bust through. His sword extended, he lunged forward toward the startled General Falcone.

Without thinking, Phillips poised the musket, eared back the cock and fired at the intruder. The weapon discharged with an almighty crash in the close confines of the room, and the swordsman was knocked to the floor, dead before he hit the tiles. A slender cavalry officer rushed forward to skewer Phillips with his sword, but Hendricks was ready with his own and slashed the officer's arm, disabling him.

As Falcone stood there in horror, his world crashing, Hendricks began speaking urgent Italian to him. Finally, Falcone gained control of himself and began shouting orders. A group of Italian soldiers came in the room and escorted Phillips and Hendricks to the shore, where Aurora's launch, lying just off the beach, came in and took them off. Before getting out of vocal range, Falcone came to the shore and began shouting at them.

As they were rowed out to the ship, Phillips ordered Hendricks to explain what had occurred back at the headquarters.

"That was General Cadorno you killed there. He had received word of the extraction and raced here with an advance guard of cavalry. When I saw Falcone disintegrating, I told him he was now in command of the Legion and must take control of them immediately before the senior officers began discussing matters. He saw my point and assured me he would send an aide to the units of the Legion based at Nakskov and order them here. The excuse being an attempted coup which he has foiled."

"Only those people in the room know exactly what happened. Fortunately, the only ones we need worry about are the few private soldiers serving as guards as well as Cadorno's aide that I wounded. I am certain Falcone has realized the importance of either silencing these men or at least putting them where they will not be in a position to cause trouble."

"The commanders here will be told an irate peddler shot General Cadorno and Falcone is assuming command."

CHAPTER THIRTY

While still on the boat rowing out to Aurora, Phillips noticed signal flags flying from a three decker accompanying the transport fleet. As he scrambled up to the entry port, his new first officer was waiting for him with a message. HMS Centaur 74, Captain Martin, had signaled for Aurora's captain to come aboard.

Phillips immediately dropped back into the boat, along with Major Hendricks and made their way to the big line-of battle ship. Captain Martin greeted them at the entryway and escorted them into his cabin.

There, Major Hendricks relayed to Martin the situation as it existed on shore at the moment. After listening to the report, Martin asked for their recommendations.

Phillips said, "I submit we attempt to embark those Italian troops just as soon as we can. It would be well if we had another Italian speaker on hand besides Major Hendricks to explain to the boarding soldiers just what is happening. Perhaps it would be well if we had a disciplined force of our own ashore just in case some of these troops do not like the new arrangements. Probably we should refrain from showing them Marine uniforms. Slop clothing would be more to the occasion, I am thinking."

By the time the men had explored all of the nuances of the situation, Centaur's lookout had reported the arrival of another three decker to the fleet. Leaving the details of the extraction to the post captains far out-ranking him, Phillips went back to shore. Signal flags were now fluttering from around the fleet, and soon a bevy of barges began to head for the beach.

Major Hendricks spoke to the officer in command of the leading battalion who believed his unit should be the first to board. The leading troops began gingerly wading out to the first boat and clamber aboard. Before it was filled, another boat was ready, then another. It took the rest of the day before all of the troops present were loaded, but then the infantry battalion formerly based at Nakskov marched in at the double.

Somehow word had reached the private soldiers they were bound for Italy, and despite the misgiving of some of their officers, had made a fast march on Rodbyhavn. The cavalry and artillery units were not far behind.

Now, another dispute entered the picture. By now the transports were well filled, and Phillips told General Falcone there was no room for the horses of the cavalry and artillery units. Falcone himself was calm with this news, but several of the officers were extremely indignant. The colonel commanding the Legion's artillery was most emphatic, assuring Phillips he would open fire with his battery at the fleet, if they attempted to sail away without his horses and guns aboard.

Phillips nodded, then beckoned to Midshipman Jeffers who was being utilized as a messenger. Scribbling a message on paper, he asked the lad to take note of a house near the shore that had apparently been damaged by a storm and was now abandoned.

"Mister Jeffers, I wish you to explain to the first officer that he should open fire on that house and that house alone when I wave my handkerchief. He should dip the ensign when he is prepared to do so. I wish the guns to fire in a disciplined broadside as a means of expressing my displeasure to a few officers ashore. One broadside alone will be enough. Are we clear?"

"Aye aye sir, one broadside on the ruined house when you wave your handkerchief."

The lad's boat crawled out to Aurora, and a moment later her ensign was seen to dip.

Phillips sauntered over the Italian artillery commander who was voluably expressing his dissatisfaction with the progress of the evacuation

"Gentlemen, the good colonel had expressed his intention to fire upon the convoy should we not embark his horses and guns. I wish to demonstrate what the consequences of that action might be. As Hendricks made the translation to the officers, he looked at the target house. He could see no one about it, but asked Hendricks to have an officer send a man to look for anyone who might be hiding from a work detail inside.

When Colonel Leone indignantly refused, Phillips pulled out his handkerchief and gave it a vigorous shake. There was a moment's delay, then every gun on Alert's port side exploded in a tremendous crash. Every ball struck the target, and the old house disintegrated in a shower of flying stone and timber.

As the awestruck artillery officers stood there amazed, Phillips addressed the officer again. "You will note my ship is the smallest of the warships in the harbor. I can assure you the line-of-battle ships are much more powerful. Are you certain you wish to fire upon the convoy?"

After Hendricks finished the translation, all the officers expressed their admiration for the demonstration and assured him none of them wished to contest the Royal Navy.

Reporting back on board Centaur, Phillips delivered his hastily written report to Captain Martin. Martin expressed his provisional satisfaction, saying this would be read in the Admiralty, and he wished the handwriting was better. He then called in his clerk and asked him how long it would be before he could produce a copy that would not embarrass the ship. The clerk glanced at the document, sniffed, and allowed two hours might be enough.

After the clerk retreated to his lair, Captain Martin said, "Unless I miss my guess, Joshua Harkins will have that re-written perfectly in an hour. If you should smudge the repaired document when you sign it, Harkins will expire of frustration."

He added, "Now that we have the extraction of the Italian troops out of the way, let me tell you of the Admiral's plans for you."

"I will carry the dispatches back home aboard Centaur. She is due for a re-fit, and it was thought a ship of force would be necessary for the protection of the convoy. In addition, I will take the corvette you captured with us. She has a useful crew aboard and can also assume her role as guardian of the flock."

"Your ship Aurora, right out of the dockyard as she is, can assume her role in exploring inland waters here in the Baltic for French naval and mercantile presence."

Captain Martin reached into a battered case on his desk and extracted a document. "This will constitute your orders. Read them carefully, but the gist is that you patrol aggressively around the Baltic waters examining every ship you can."

"Some discretion is in order. Technically, we are at war with the Czar of Russia, but feelers our diplomats have extended seem to indicate his heart is no longer in a fight against us. Therefore, you should not initiate any action against Russian forces or property unless you are aggressively attacked. By the same token Bonaparte has forced Sweden to declare war against us, but it is a strange kind of war."

"Our ships, for example are free to purchase supplies in any Swedish port not protected by a battery. The Swedes do not want to fight us, but they cannot afford to antagonize Bonaparte, who would occupy their country on a whim. Again, you should defend your ship against attack, but you should not attack Swedish shipping or property, unless you are prepared to defend your actions in front of Admiral Saumarez."

"Should you need supplies, you may wish to send a boat into any Swedish port not protected by a battery, under a white flag of course, and ask permission. In any case, you will return to the fleet in two months' time and report to the flag. Any questions?"

With that, Phillips made his departure and was rowed over to Aurora. There, he invited Lieutenant Wheeler, his first officer into his cabin and explained what was going on. Wheeler was ecstatic. Losing his command had cost him important money, but now that he was on the books as first officer with the prospect of sharing in some lucrative prizes, the world seemed brighter.

Dipping her flag in salute to Captain Martin, HMS Aurora stood out into the Baltic and took up her patrol.

CHAPTER THIRTY ONE

The shipping in the Baltic was a confusing variety, some of which he was required to attack, while other national ships he must not. As explained to him previously, while Britain was at war with Russia and Sweden, he must not attack their shipping or shore installations. Danish and French ships and facilities were proper targets and should be pursued by fervor. Other shipping, from some of the German nations, for example might better be approached with caution.

Not wishing to put himself in a situation where he could be pursued in civil litigation, he resolved to spend most of his efforts on French and Danish shipping, although he decided he could examine the cargo of other, more questionably flagged ships. Should he find a merchant ship with a military cargo consigned to a French controlled port, he felt he could seize that ship with no recriminations.

His first capture on this voyage was an easy one. The weather was mild, at the moment, and he ordered the men off watch to sleep at their guns, in this target rich area. They had barely sunk the topsails of the fleet below the horizon, when right around a point jutting out from a Danish island came a big schooner. The lookout shouted the sighting but nearly everyone on the ship saw it at about the same time.

Looking over at his starboard battery, Phillips saw the gun captain on number four gun had most of his crew ready. Ordering Mister Wheeler to clear for action, Phillips walked over to number four gun and asked Ploughman there if he could put a ball across the schooner's bow. "Now I don't want you to hit her, Ploughman. She is flying no flag and we do not want to hurt somebody if she is not a legitimate target. "

"Aye aye, sir. Close, it is."

"That is the spirit Ploughman. If you can convince that schooner to stop without hitting her, every man on your gun will get an extra tot of grog tonight."

The gun crew had heard all the words and were now diligently on duty at their stations. The gun was already loaded, so the only thing to do was to cast loose the gun from its fastenings and open the port lid. The tompion was removed from the muzzle from the muzzle while the gunner installed the flintlock firing mechanism, inspecting the flint and checking for the presence of dampness in the pan. He rammed his priming pin into the touch hole to insure a clear passage for ignition and shoved a priming quill into the touch hole.

With his crew all at their stations he glanced at his Captain. Phillips said, "You may fire when you are quite ready, Ploughman."

The gunner stood behind the gun peering down the barrel, judging how the gun was pointed, estimating the elevation and trying to predict the action of the sea on the ship. Quietly, he instructed his men to shift the gun a touch to port. He decided not to worry about elevation since the ship was rolling with the sea, so he would just have to wait for the right moment before he fired.

Ploughman also had to consider exactly how far the gun would recoil upon firing. He had made a tiny nick in the deck with his knife which the first lieutenant had never noticed. He knew as long as he stood behind that mark, the gun would not strike him.

With everything considered and the ship at the top of her roll, Ploughman guessed their time was right. He gave his lanyard a yank and the gun fired with a roar, sending the iron beast crashing back against the breeching ropes. The gun stopped its recoil just inches before reaching his body. He had trained his mind over the years to appear to ignore that two tons of iron crashing toward his face.

Every time he pulled that lanyard he was terrified, but no one ever guessed. This time the ball struck the sea a fathom before the schooner's cutwater. The men of the crew made sounds of admiration but he knew he had erred. He had meant to place the ball another fathom forward.

Phillips was pleased, though. As the schooner came into the wind, and waited for boarding, Phillips said, "You and your crew have earned your tot. You will get it tonight. I appreciate your abilities."

The schooner had a mixed cargo of iron bars, pork in casks and sawn timber. All valuable contents which would bring a good price. The schooner itself was registered as French with a French captain. Her crew came from differing nations. There were Poles, Danes, some Swedes and even a Hanoverian German.

When these crewmen realized they were destined for the prison hulks that lined some of the harbors in Britain, many volunteered for duty with the Baltic Fleet. After all, they were seamen and duty on one ship was much the same as another. Actually, duty on a Royal Navy ship was often easier, since there were usually more men available to do work than on merchant craft. Those who would not accept recruitment were taken below and put in irons until Chips could construct a place to hold them.

With the prize inventoried, her seamen removed, a minimal prize crew was selected for her and she was given to a proud midshipman to command. A long-service bosun's mate was put aboard to offer advice when needed to the mid, and her crew made preparations to sail her back to the fleet.

Phillips took the mid to the quarterdeck to give him some advice. He assured him a commander never had enough knowledge and there was no stigma against receiving it. He reminded Mister Wilson he would indeed be in command, but Bosun's Mate Atkins was aboard for a reason, and if it were found the prize or its crew suffered for Mister Wilson failing to avail himself of some information from Wilson, the mid would have a very short career in the Navy indeed.

After watching the schooner sail off, Phillips set Aurora off on the hunt again. The next traffic encountered were a few fishermen in a heavy fore-and-aft rigged shallop. They were hand-line fishing for cod from open boats, three of them, it appeared. It being obvious the shallop carried no military supplies, Phillips did not bother them but had a Swedish crewman ask if they wished to sell any fish. The men were not averse to the silver shillings he offered, and some fine cod were hoisted aboard to relieve the steady diet of boiled salt beef and boiled salt pork.

Now the ship headed toward the Mecklenburg coast. This region was a member of the Confederation of the Rhine and allied with Bonaparte. As she neared the coast, the sloop began sighting various coasting vessels. Sailing under Danish colors, Phillips let the first few coasters go by, since he felt they were not worth bothering with. Soon though, a heavily laden brig was encountered. Deep in the water, she was too slow to escape Aurora. Although she had a dozen old guns aboard, she did not have enough crew to fight and hauled down her flag as soon as the first ball slashed in front of her bow.

A Mecklenburg ship bound for Copenhagen with a cargo of wheat was a legitimate prize and Phillips sent her to Admiral Saumarez. He realized he could not keep sending in prizes, since he had few people he could use as prize masters. He had exactly two mids left and he would not trust either with the key to the tea caddy, let alone a valuable prize.

For another month he ranged through the northern Baltic, burning prize after prize, to the ever increasing discontent of his crew. Every capture his men saw go up in smoke, they regarded as money from their pockets burning.

It was now late in the fall and the weather was becoming increasingly cold. Ice was forming in the bays and protected inlets, and soon he must make the decision to leave,

He was debating the subject with himself when they spotted a big, ship-rigged vessel. Flying no flag, she cut over to the east to try to reach a safe harbor before Aurora came up to her, but to no avail. This ship was laden with new cannon barrels, of the French 'huit' (eight pounder) caliber. Again there was no question about this ship. She was French owned and registered and she was bound for Brest along the Atlantic coast.

Phillips felt the owners must have been very optimistic to carry such a cargo out of the Baltic, into the North Sea then through the Channel to

Brest in a sea swarming with British raiders. Whatever the reason, the gun now belonged to the Navy and Phillips was not about to give them up easily. He sent Mister Wheeler, his first officer over to command the ship and gave him enough men to sail her. He had left in Aurora only his Master's Mate, and a pair of very young mids to lead the crew.

This was as good an excuse as anything else he could think of to sail back to the fleet. It was a week before they found HMS Victory in the Gulf of Finland. The weather was frigid and spray was constantly freezing on the decks and rigging. Ice was advancing more every day in the water and Admiral Saumarez apparently felt it was now time to leave.

It was a bitterly cold night when they traversed the narrow Oresund on their way out of the Baltic. At its narrowest, between Kronberg Castle at Helsingor in Danish Zeeland and Helsingborg in Sweden, the strait is only a bit over two miles wide. It was just possible to make there passage through the gap, with the wind as it was. Normally the Danish gunners at Helsingor would have been only too happy to salute the convoy with iron balls as they sailed by, but apparently those gunners were all asleep in their beds.

The battery commanders might be excused for letting their gunners have the night off, since the weather was so frightful. Of course, it should have been known that mad Englishmen were apt to go out in all kinds of weather. When Victory sailed by, she saluted the batteries with a few broadsides from her portside guns.

As Aurora sailed south with the convoy the weather warmed a bit so at least the men did not have to spend every watch breaking ice from the deck and rigging. Phillips had had just about enough of this cold weather sailing. He well knew the Navy would not let his ship sit idle all winter, but there was always the possibility of going back to the Med, or even across to the Caribbean.

It would be grand if he could find the time to go to the family estate in Essex and see his sister and just possibly his father. The latter visit would be at long odds against, since Phillips Pater was also a captain, a post captain in this case.

He expected some of his previous prizes might have been adjudicated by now and the funds released. Perhaps he should think about purchasing an estate as hiis father had done?